Dear Reader

At the top of New Zealand's South Island is Blenheim, set in a beautiful area with vineyards for as far as you can see and then some. The Wither Hills make a stunning backdrop, and the waters of the Wairau River seem to change colour depending on the season.

It is the perfect place for Erin and Brad to meet and fall in love. If only life was that easy. Both have painful pasts to deal with before they can find happiness. When Brad is forced back home he dreads facing his past, but being thrown into working with Erin leaves him no room for running away again.

I apologise to Lucky, the cat, for the role I have given her in this story. In real life she would never have done such a thing. I am thrilled to have finished this, my third Medical™ Romance. I hope you enjoy reading Brad and Erin's story.

Cheers!

Sue MacKay

www.suemackay.co.nz

With a background working in medical laboratories, and a love of the romance genre, it is no surprise that **Sue MacKay** writes Medical™ Romance stories. An avid reader all her life, she wrote her first story at age eight—about a prince, of course. She lives with her husband in beautiful Marlborough Sounds, at the top of New Zealand's South Island, where she can indulge her passions for the outdoors, the sea and cycling. She is currently training as a volunteer ambulance officer.

RETURN OF
THE MAVERICK

BY
SUE MacKAY

First published in Great Britain 2011
by Mills & Boon, an imprint of Harlequin (UK) Limited.
Large Print edition 2012
Harlequin (UK) Limited, Eton House,
18-24 Paradise Road, Richmond, Surrey TW9 1SR

© Sue MacKay 2011

ISBN: 978 0 263 22436 8

Harlequin (UK) policy is to use papers that are
natural, renewable and recyclable products and made
from wood grown in sustainable forests. The logging
and manufacturing process conform to the legal
environmental regulations of the country of origin.

Printed and bound in Great Britain
by CPI Antony Rowe, Chippenham, Wiltshire

Also by Sue MacKay:

PLAYBOY DOCTOR TO DOTING DAD
THEIR MARRIAGE MIRACLE

**Did you know these are also available as eBooks?
Visit www.millsandboon.co.uk**

Dedicated to the girlfriends—
Faye, Fay, Jill & Jen.
For the wine and coffees, laughter and tears,
and your amazing support 2010/11.

CHAPTER ONE

'WHAT time did you set out biking this morning?' the woman behind the counter asked as she totted up how much Erin Foley owed for her groceries.

'Six.' Erin rolled her shoulders, the muscles tight from bending over the handlebars. Her body felt warm, taut, fit. A hot shower would cap off a great ride and prepare her for the day ahead at the medical centre.

Savita shook her head. 'You're nuts. Sane people are still in bed at that hour.'

Erin grinned. 'You were here when I went past on my way out.' Scooping up the milk and pot of margarine, she pushed them into her backpack. Glancing at her watch, she scowled. 'First day back from my holidays and I'm going to be late for work.' First day working with the new GP. However temporary he was, he probably wouldn't be impressed with her tardiness.

Not unless he was also a cyclist, and understood the need to train for mountain bike challenges. But she already knew he rode a Harley rather than pedalling an Avanti. Did he ride his motorbike to work? Take it on house calls? That would have the patients talking. Less chance of being late with a Harley too.

Savita laughed. 'You caught me out. I got here just after five-thirty.'

'And you think I'm nuts? See you tomorrow.' Erin grabbed her bread, spun around and ran slap bang into someone standing right behind her. The loaf of bread fell from her fingers as she strove to keep her balance. Her other hand slapped against hard chest muscle.

Large hands gripped her upper arms. 'Easy,' growled a deep voice from somewhere above her head.

Erin instantly stepped back against the counter, trying to ignore the broad chest filling her sight. The stranger dropped his hands immediately. Shifting sideways, she tried to manoeuvre around him, but he moved at the same moment in the same direction. Briefly they danced around each other, trying to pass, until Erin stopped. 'Your move.'

She flipped her head back to say more and blinked. Not because of the harsh summer sunlight streaming through the door, although with the morning temperature already in the midtwenties that was glaring enough. No. It was the man standing right in front of her who'd taken her breath away.

The strikingly big man.

His white cotton shirt contrasted with the tanned skin of his throat, and was tucked into casual navy-blue trousers that fitted his hips and thighs to perfection. Her lungs squeezed, tried to take in air as he reached down to pick up her dropped loaf.

'Your bread.' Amusement laced that bass tone.

'Thank you.' Snatching the plastic-wrapped loaf from his extended hand, she shoved it into her backpack before slinging it over her shoulders, determined not to stare. But she failed. Noted how his arms now folded over his chest accentuated everything underneath that shirt. Lots of well-honed muscles pushed out the crisp fabric.

Erin swallowed with difficulty. Forced herself to look away. Unfortunately her gaze dropped, down to those thighs. Dear heaven. A sharp ache snagged her bottom lip where her teeth bit in. Sweat trickled down between her shoulder blades. Her fingers shook so that she had trouble getting the two ends of the pack's straps to click together across her abdomen.

Men were not supposed to look like this. Good enough to eat. More than good enough to want go to bed with.

You don't know who he is. And you want to sleep with him?

She blinked again, trying to blot out the image of him sprawled across her king-size bed. As if that worked. It would take more strength than she possessed to mentally delete that picture. Giving in to temptation, she continued her downward perusal. Big feet.

Another swallow.

If she turned back to Savita and tried leaving again, would she find he'd been a figment of her imagination? An illusion brought on by a drought of close contact with the male species?

She had dated a few times over the previous year, to test the water and expel some of the loneliness that dogged her. But even now that her guilt about her husband, Jonathon, had started ebbing away there was still the fear of losing her carefully gained control over her life. That tended to deter her from any serious relationship she might be interested in starting. The need to be in charge of her life was a big part of why she'd left the army two years ago; why she'd moved to the South Island and Blenheim rather than return to Auckland where she'd done her nursing degree; why she'd bought her very own house and planted a garden.

'You said something about being late.' The man's voice matched his body. Big. Toned. Sexy.

'Yes, I am,' she answered. And getting later by the minute. But her feet were still anchored to the floor. A tremor ran through her. If she couldn't move because of her knee-weakening attraction to this man, then she was in serious trouble. When was the last time she'd ever felt as though her skin was crackling because of a man? That had never happened. Not once. Not even Jonathon had managed to have that effect on her.

He was handing money to Savita for a newspaper, but watching her. 'Do you usually go for long rides before work?'

Tugging her spine straight and her shoulders back, Erin looked directly up at his face. Sunglasses covered his eyes. But goose-bumps still lifted on her arms. His sun-bleached blond hair touched his shoulders. A scar ran from his bottom lip to his chin. His strong jaw line jutted challengingly. She could almost feel that mouth on her feverish skin.

She stammered an answer, 'I—I'm training for a b-bike challenge that goes over a mountain pass down into Hanmer Springs.'

'Sounds like hard work to me.' He grinned at her, sending her stomach into a riot of spasms.

'I enjoy it.' She would not grab the counter for support. He'd notice and she didn't want him to see how easily he'd rattled her. It was a senseless overreaction. He was a stranger and likely to stay that way. She'd never seen him anywhere around Blenheim, a small town where he'd have been noticed the moment he stepped outside his front door. And not just by her. He was a man that every female alive would notice. And would want. But for her he was out of bounds. Even a brief fling would mean giving up some of that control she valued so much. Damn it, she could already feel it slipping away and she'd been in his presence less than five minutes.

She headed outside and reached for her bike. He followed, the newspaper tucked under his arm. When she swung her leg over the seat his eyes tracked the movement, raising her heart beat to a ridiculously high rate for an extremely fit thirty-year-old. Keep this up and she'd fall off before she'd even got to the road. 'I might see you around,' she muttered, but didn't pull out onto the bitumen.

Why was she making conversation with him? She didn't know his name. And she didn't need these strong and alien feelings of desire he'd switched on in her. A man like this would wake up the dead with his sexual allure, and she was only emotionally paralysed. She certainly didn't want to grapple with the overwhelming guilt and pain of the past again.

But she couldn't deny the bone-melting desire he'd turned on as easily as flicking a light switch. Her blood already hummed through her veins, sending tendrils of heat down to her toes, out to her fingers.

'We could meet for a drink.' His eyes lanced her, the warm colour of creamy fudge.

From somewhere deep inside Erin dredged up a reply. 'Thanks, but I don't think so.' Not what her hormones were telling her, but what the sane and sensible side of her brain deemed was in her best interests.

'Really?' he drawled. He stood next to her, dwarfing her, which at five-eight wasn't something she was used to.

Had he seen through her precarious self-control? 'I really need to get going. I'll be more than just a few minutes late for work now.' She didn't wait for his reply, instead pushed hard on the pedals and cycled down the footpath until a gap in the traffic allowed her onto the road.

But while she might be outwardly casually dismissing this guy, she wasn't fooling herself. He was hot. And her body reacted to him like kittens to a saucer of milk. She wanted him.

She wasn't having him.

Besides, right now she should be at home preparing for work and her first meeting with the man she'd once told in no uncertain terms over the phone that he was letting down someone very dear to her. The man who had started work at the medical centre last week while she'd been on holiday and whom she had to get on with if she was to keep the job that gave her so much satisfaction.

But who was that guy back at the shop?

Brad Perano knew he should've turned away the moment he saw her slide off the bike and straighten up. As she strode into the store her long legs had immediately snagged his attention. The attraction had been instant. He'd followed her without thinking about what he was doing. Who knew which paper he'd bought? He'd just grabbed blindly.

Next she'd be having him up on charges for stalking her if he wasn't careful. *Really?* his brain taunted him as he watched her pedal away. She'd been interested in him too. He'd seen it in her widening eyes, in the way her teeth had bitten into her lip, in the dazed expression she'd worn as she'd tried to buckle that strap.

But she'd had more sense than him. She'd said no to his reckless suggestion of a drink together. He owed her for that. But he was flummoxed that he'd even asked the woman out when he'd vowed never to get close to any female again. Hadn't he learned the lessons dearest Penelope had taught him so well? The one and only time he'd allowed himself to be vulnerable, his wife had gobbled him up like a hungry dog and spewed out the resulting mess years later.

The bright red helmet the woman wore was easy to follow as she weaved her way through the busy morning traffic. Then she turned a corner and he lost sight of her. Which was just as well. He'd intended getting to the clinic early to familiarise himself with the day's patients. He didn't like treating people without knowing their medical history thoroughly. He'd known some of these people when he'd lived here in New Zealand's beautiful Marlborough district as a child; gone to school with them, partied, played rugby. Real friends he'd dumped on and left in the lurch.

To patients in a small community their doctor was a part of their lives. Now he had to get to know them all over again and hope they were willing to give him a second chance. Then there was the added humiliation of Penelope's perfidy after she'd flaunted her extravagant lifestyle in their faces years ago. Would they treat him kindly? Or was he always going to be paying for his misspent youth and his crazy marriage?

Car tyres squealed. The sound came from the direction the woman had ridden. More screeches rent the air as other drivers slammed on brakes. A scream chilled Brad's blood. Had she been hit? Car versus cyclist did not bode well. He'd seen that kind of accident all too often in Adelaide where he'd been living and working for the last three years. The cyclists always came off worst.

He ran.

As he turned the corner he saw a mangled bike lying in the middle of the road. Three people gathered around a body lying twisted in the wreckage.

A bright red helmet caught his focus. And the breath he'd been holding eased out over his lips. The woman was kneeling beside a young child, her fingers on his wrist.

She was all right. The relief was immense and surprising. Even as he made his way to her side and knelt down he was questioning why he felt so charged around her.

She looked up, and her eyes widened as they had at the store. 'I've called the ambulance but I don't suppose by any chance you might be a doctor?'

'It's your lucky day. I am.' He felt good to be able to say that, giving her what she wanted right at this moment.

'Lucky day for the boy, not me. I didn't really think I had a chance of my wish being granted.' She turned to the child and concentrated on finding a pulse.

Oh, well, okay. She was thinking about the patient, which was exactly what he should be doing. Once again she'd distracted him. 'How's that pulse?'

'It's racing.' She ran her free hand over the boy's torso. 'Hey, little man, can you hear me? I'm a nurse and I'm checking you over, okay?' She got no answer.

A racing pulse indicated shock. Not surprising considering that the boy seemed to have been knocked off his bike by a small van. Brad studied the scene, noting the bike's back wheel wrapped around the child's leg, an arm lying at an odd angle indicating a fracture, and blood streaming from his forehead. He appeared unconscious. Brad delicately felt the young boy's head for trauma injuries.

He turned to the nurse. 'There's a major contusion on the right-hand side of the head.' Brain injury was a serious consideration.

'Can we remove the bike without moving him?' she asked.

'You're thinking of spinal injuries.' He studied the way the boy's foot was through the spokes. 'We could but it's best we wait for the paramedics so they can put a collar on first.'

They worked together, quickly and carefully, checking the boy thoroughly. Within moments an ambulance pulled up and a paramedic was with them. 'Hey, what've we got?'

Brad quickly explained the injuries he'd noted while the paramedic applied a plastic collar, his gaze returning to the boy. Blond hair was plastered to the boy's scalp. Brad's belly suddenly clenched. The young innocent face, now very pale, dredged up a memory from deep in Brad's soul.

Raw pain sliced through him, wrenched his heart. 'Sammy.' The name tore through him, spilled over his tongue, out into the street. 'Sammy.'

His beloved boy hurting, his body broken, not moving at all. Sammy could be dying. He could have a serious brain injury. And his father couldn't help him.

The nurse had a hand on his wrist, shaking him, talking to him in a calm voice. 'Doctor, this is Jason Curtis. He lives just along the road.'

'What?' Brad dragged his gaze from the lad and turned to stare into the sincerest, deepest blue eyes he'd ever seen. The woman was telling him something important. He shook his head in an attempt to clear away the fog, and listened carefully.

'Jason Curtis. His father works at the building centre.' She dropped his wrist.

'Not Sammy?' Not his son? Hope flared. Brad looked back at the boy lying before him, and gulped. He looked nothing like Samuel. Except for the blond hair, the skinny legs and knobbly knees. Brad's head spun. Damn it, he'd just made an idiot of himself freaking out like that. How could it be Samuel anyway? He was far away in California. The pain subsided, and Brad leaned down to run the back of his hand over the boy's soft cheek, his fingers shaking.

Not his son, but another man would be feeling this agony as soon as he learned about the accident. What did these medical people think of *him* losing his cool like that? They'd probably cart him off to the lock up if he wasn't careful. He looked around at the thinning crowd. At least no one here seemed to have recognised him. Thank goodness. He didn't want his mistake added to the rest of the gossip no doubt circulating around Blenheim about him. Twisting his neck further, he found the nurse's thoughtful gaze on him. She'd heard every word he'd uttered.

She gave him a tentative smile before filling in the patient report form for the ambulance crew. 'Jason's mum works in ED.'

The second officer leaned over and read the boy's name. He whistled. 'This is Polly's boy? She's already on shift.'

Glad of the distraction, Brad said, 'Tricky. What happens when you call this job through to ED? It could be her who picks up the radio link.' He felt for the woman. 'Is there any other way of letting the staff know so they can tell her personally?'

'We'll phone in on our cell,' one of the medics answered as he strapped the oxygen mask to Jason. 'Right, let's get that bike off and roll this lad onto the backboard.'

The four of them worked to get Jason safely untangled before transferring him to the stretcher and into the ambulance.

Brad turned to the nurse now standing beside him. 'Phew, I'm glad that's over. I always feel uncomfortable dealing with these situations when I've got no equipment at hand.'

'I know exactly what you mean.' Her teeth dug into her bottom lip. 'And poor Polly's going to get a shock, even if she is told before Jason gets there.' She looked up at him and he could see the thought in her eyes.

A shock such as he'd just had.

Stepping up to the back of the ambulance, the woman advised the paramedic, 'Tell Polly I've gone round to tell Jason's father, will you?'

The paramedic began closing the back of the ambulance. 'Sure will. And thanks for your help, Erin. I wish you'd come and join us. You'd make a great team member and we could use your skills.'

Brad gasped. Erin? As in Erin Foley, nurse at the medical centre he'd started working at? What would she have to say about his loss of concentration back there? If she informed the staff at the centre about it they might think they had more cause to look at him sideways.

But right now she was saying with an expressive shrug, 'Who knows? If my new boss doesn't work out, I might have to consider it.'

Still absorbing this latest bombshell, Brad muttered, 'You've got doubts about a new boss before you've even worked with him?' Why? Could she be feeling remorse for the tongue-lashing she'd given him over the phone last month despite not knowing him?

Erin blinked at him. 'Ah, yes, I have.' Turning her shoulder to him, she spoke to the paramedic again.

Of course she'd think it was none of Brad's business. He should tell her who he was, get whatever was bothering her out in the open before clinic began. But, damn it, this was the woman who'd forced his hand, made him jump on a plane and cross the Tasman to help out the man who'd taken care of him years ago. If not for Erin Foley's caustic phone call he'd still be justifying staying in Adelaide, pretending it was work that kept him there, not reluctance to face a town full of people who'd despised him for being a bad boy as a teenager. People who were no doubt laughing up their sleeves at his failed marriage, thinking he'd got his just deserts for believing he could escape his roots and rubbing their noses in it as he went. He shivered. And he couldn't bear if they started in on Samuel.

The laughter about his mistakes and misdemeanours he could handle, but if anyone dared say a word about Samuel's parentage he wouldn't be able to hold in his hurt and anger.

A nudge in the arm from Erin's elbow brought him back to his surroundings. She asked politely, 'Are you okay? You look a bit pale.'

Pale? 'I'm fine.' He opened his clenched hands. 'You want me to come with you to tell the boy's father?'

'No, thanks. I know them well.'

And he was a stranger. In her eyes, at least. There was a very real chance he'd know one of Jason's parents, might've gone to school with one of them, so it was best he didn't go with Erin to see Jason's father. Brad didn't want the past getting in the way of what she had to tell the other man. 'Fair enough. Though someone else might've already beaten you to the door.'

'Very likely but I need to make sure. I'd say Jason was on his way to school when he was hit by the van.' She stretched her legs and looked around the crowd, nodded at a few people she obviously knew.

Of course she knew them. Some of them might even be patients at the medical centre where he now worked. Where she worked. He was her boss and he was interested in her other than as a nurse. That had to stop right now. This very instant. It wasn't professional.

Only last week when he'd started at the clinic he'd had to hold his tongue when everyone had told him about the competent and cheerful nurse who had gone on leave the same day he'd started. He'd known the acid of her tongue over the phone, but nothing else about her. He'd expected a middle-aged paragon who was efficiency personified. No one had told him she was drop-dead gorgeous, and that was with a helmet on and wearing those dreadful Spandex cycle shorts with the padded seat.

Movement out of the corner of Brad's eye caught his attention. Two youngsters were picking up a bike from the side of the road, a bike that looked suspiciously like Erin's. 'Hey, you two.'

The boys stopped, glanced over their shoulders, apprehension on their sulky faces. Little blighters had been about to steal the bike. 'Put that down now.'

Their apprehension grew, but they remained quiet.

Erin looked around. 'What's going on?'

'Those two were borrowing your bike.' He'd managed to stop their silly escapade.

Her head spun around so fast she had to be giddy. Her eyes hardened, and she stormed across to retrieve her cycle. Damn, but she looked even more beautiful when she was angry. Something he didn't need to know. But his brain seemed to be filing it away for later anyway.

She growled at the boys in a low voice that stroked his raw nerves. 'You were going to steal my bike? How dare you? If you want a bike, get a job and earn the money for one. I should report you to the police.'

One of the boys scoffed, 'Yeah, right, lady.'

The other glared at her defensively. 'Who'd give us a job?'

She looked from one boy to the other, a frown scrunching her forehead. 'I would, if I could. Unfortunately there aren't any jobs for schoolkids where I work.'

Brad noted how hope flared quickly in the lads' eyes, and disappeared as rapidly. Poor kids. Maybe he could think of something. But in the meantime they still owed her an apology. He turned to the boys. 'Haven't you two got something to say to this lady?'

Like twins they screwed their noses into sneers and rolled their eyes at her. But they did mutter, 'Sorry.'

'I imagine that's as good as I'm going to get.'

He sighed. He'd heard these sorts of comments throughout his youth. People always expected the worst of kids from the wrong part of town, and judging by the worn and ill-fitting school uniforms these two were wearing, that was exactly where they came from. 'You could give them a break.'

'What? Am I supposed to congratulate the boys for being would-be thieves? They need a good dressing down.'

True, and they'd get one from him if their parents weren't forthcoming. Did he know these boys' families? It might be better for him if he left them alone and headed straight to the clinic. *Don't get involved. Don't stir up the past any more than you have to.*

But he still shook his head at Erin in warning

before turning to the boys. 'Come on, you two. Let's get out of here.'

Before he hauled this woman into his arms, bike and all, and kissed her until her legs couldn't hold her up. Banging his hand on his head, he muttered, 'What the hell's the matter with me?'

He tried to concentrate on the lads, tried to ignore her as she checked the road was clear before cycling away. She was going to be furious when she learned who he was. Why hadn't he introduced himself once he'd realised they'd be working together?

Because he didn't want to see the disdain at what she perceived to be his lack of compassion towards David any sooner than he had to. Had she heard about his bad-boy reputation? Would that add to her scorn?

But as those trim legs pumped the pedals he couldn't stop staring after her. His hungry gaze followed her out onto the road. Her backside, clad in those cycling shorts, was a sight not to be missed. It sent his temperature soaring, his heart racing, and his groin aching. He really tried to look elsewhere, for his own sake, but he couldn't.

He watched as she weaved amongst the traffic, his gaze following her until she finally disappeared from sight.

Unfortunately he couldn't disappear off the radar for the next few months as he'd committed to helping David adjust to his illness. That took precedence over everything. Over everyone, including blue-eyed beauties. The same one who'd rightly accused him during that phone conversation of putting David second.

Home. The one place he'd been too ashamed to return to. The place he and his ex-wife had been in a hurry to leave and make a fresh start away from his bad image. Away to a city where he didn't have to explain to a patient that while he might've stolen a shirt off their washing line years earlier, he could now competently diagnose their illness. In Adelaide his wife had finally begun to carve out the lifestyle she'd craved all her underprivileged childhood. Brad had always known Penelope had used him to get out of Blenheim but he'd understood her, and loved her enough to give her what she wanted. Big mistake.

His marriage had been the one subject that had

been taboo between him and David. The older man had seen further ahead than Brad could, had known no one could feed Penelope's hunger. David had foreseen no amount of wealth would give her what she needed, and he'd argued long and hard with Brad not to marry her. Brad had believed he could provide more than enough to keep his wife happy. Time had proved David right, Brad wrong, and cost him his son.

He and David had patched the rift between them enough to get along again, but the deep affection they'd always known since David had first taken him into his home as a fourteen-year-old was missing. The man who'd kept him out of court, made him accountable for his own actions and, finally, set him on the right path to a successful career now needed looking out for.

Brad glanced at the two boys skulking along beside him. He'd expected they'd have taken off by now. 'You two hungry?'

Two heads flicked around, astonishment in their eyes. 'Yes.'

'Okay, back to the shop. I saw some buns and

sandwiches in a cabinet that should fill the hole in your bellies.'

'Cool.'

'Thanks, man.'

'Call me Brad.' His step lightened. He liked it that he could do something for those that life gave a rough deal. He put on his confident, competent doctor's face, the one that hid his nervousness about facing up to people he'd hurt in the past.

Then there was Erin. He had to front up to her too. At least she hadn't featured in his past. Neither was she going to feature in his future. Settling into David's place in the practice had just got a whole load more difficult.

CHAPTER TWO

ERIN rushed into the medical centre as though being chased by a hungry lion, knowing she'd have kept a lot of people waiting. She had an immunisation clinic and the waiting room was full of young mothers and their toddlers. 'Sorry I'm late, everyone, but there was an accident and I stopped to give a hand.'

'It's okay, we heard,' one of the women said as she shoved a pacifier in the mouth of a screeching child.

A curly-haired toddler grabbed at the hem of Erin's straight denim skirt, tugging her to a halt.

'Hey, gorgeous, how are you today?' Erin bent down and swung Katie Bryant into her arms.

Big brown eyes stared back at her out of a pale face with shadows on her cheeks. One tiny fist tapped Erin's chin.

'I guess that means you're fine.' Erin kissed the

top of Katie's head and gently placed her back on her feet. 'Is she not sleeping too well?' she asked Alison, Katie's mother.

'Too much sometimes. I never have trouble putting her to bed these days.'

Maybe she was overreacting but Erin decided she'd get Annie or Dr Perano to take a look at Katie before her injection. The little girl didn't look quite right, not as robust as she usually was. A temperature reading wouldn't go astray either. Glancing around the room, Erin's heart squeezed as she saw all the little ones playing and crying and chattering, the mums talking and laughing as though they had all the time in the world. This was what she wanted, more than anything else. To be a mother, to have her own family. This was what she could never have.

She may have reconciled herself to the fact that she was infertile but that hadn't stopped the hurt, the fierce need or the raw longing that sometimes overtook her. Especially on days like this when she worked with lots of children.

Infertility sucked.

Erin leaned over the counter at Reception, looking for the pile of files relating to her young patients. She said quietly to the receptionist, 'Jason Curtis was hit by a car. Has anything come through from the hospital about his condition yet?'

Marilyn paused between phone calls. 'Dr Perano said he'd ring ED shortly. He told us you'd been there so we figured you'd be running behind time.'

'Dr Perano? How would he know—?' Erin's stomach dropped. 'The guy at the accident scene was a doctor… *That* was Bradley Perano?'

Embarrassment gripped her, making her squirm right down to her sandals. She'd been ogling him at the corner store. What was that going to do for their future working relationship? She gaped at Marilyn. 'No way. That couldn't have been Dr Perano. Too much of a coincidence.'

Please, she silently begged the receptionist, *please tell me I'm wrong in my supposition.*

'Definitely me.' A deep, sexy voice came from behind the door of the office where the filing cabinets stood. He appeared in the middle of the office, taking up all the space with his big frame. 'But not really a coincidence when you think we weren't far from the clinic. I was on my way here when I stopped at the store.'

Here, where they were to work together. Did he also know that by living with Dr David Taylor he'd become her neighbour too? Breathe. Slowly. In. Out. Erin spied the patient notes she needed as she turned to face Dr Perano fully. 'So you've guessed I'm Erin, the practice nurse?'

He came to shake her hand. 'Yes, I worked it out when that paramedic used your name.'

'You didn't say anything.' Her hand disappeared somewhere inside his big, rough one.

His expression turned wary, but he said in the voice that made her heart rate speed up, 'Sorry about that, but there was a lot going on.'

Sure, there had been, but there'd also been ample opportunity to introduce himself. 'It would've been nice if you'd said something. We tend to be friendly around here.' And she could've prepared herself better for this moment.

Wariness turned to disbelief. 'I'm sure you're right.' His tone suggested otherwise. 'Anyway, now we've met. Everyone talked you up big time last week. You and Annie.'

Annie was her best friend and a part-time GP at the medical centre. They'd spent a week in Golden Bay with Annie's three little boys while Annie's husband had been overseas with his job as a wine-maker.

'Annie's wonderful. Her patients love her.' With a start Erin realised Brad was still holding her hand. A nervous tug and she'd retrieved it. She jammed her hand in the big pocket on her skirt, holding in the warmth he'd engendered. If only she'd had known who this guy was before making an idiot of herself at the shop. She'd heard so much about him from David that she'd made the mis-take of thinking she already knew him. Never in her wildest dreams had she imagined a man so imposing that she lost all sense of reality around him. It was only day one. She'd get over this by tomorrow and then they'd work together without any problems.

She was very happy at this medical centre where she'd got to know the patients, and the staff treated her like one of their own. She did not need anyone disrupting that.

Bradley was still talking, no contrition in his voice. 'I've heard your patients adore you, too.'

Ignoring that she edged around him, muttering, 'Excuse me, but I need to get working.'

Stepping in front of her, he stopped her escape. 'Erin, can I have a word first? In my office?'

'Can it wait, Dr Perano? I've held up these people long enough already.' She looked around the waiting room and was astonished to see all the mothers watching her and obviously listening to their conversation.

'Firstly, it's Brad, not Dr Perano. Secondly...' And the guy paused to smile beguilingly across at those waiting women. 'Secondly, I'm sure no one will mind if I talk to my practice nurse for a few minutes.'

'Go ahead.' One mother grinned. 'He's far more interesting than us lot.'

Thanks a million. Where was female solidarity when you needed it? Erin scowled at them all and only got winks and grins back. Except from Alison Byrant, who seemed to be studying the new doctor carefully.

In Brad's office Erin sat, waiting, on the corner

of his desk. What did he want to talk to her about that couldn't be said out in the office? Goosebumps lifted the skin on her arms. Probably that phone conversation when she'd told him how selfish she thought he was for not coming home to give David some support.

Now that the Parkinson's disease that had struck David was relentlessly getting worse, it was time for Brad to pay his dues. That night when she'd answered the phone for David after cleaning him up she had been fit to yell at someone. Bradley Perano had phoned at the perfect time. She mightn't have met him back then but she'd certainly told him what she thought of him. Her heart thudded slowly and painfully. She had been abrupt and he'd deserved better. He had his own problems, which David had alluded to but not divulged.

Apprehension trickled across her mind as she watched this insanely good-looking man close the door firmly and make his way around to sit behind his desk, his long legs taking few strides to reach his chair. Light scuff marks showed on his trousers where he'd knelt down on the road beside her to attend to Jason.

Erin swivelled around, keeping him in sight. Her gaze was drawn to his fingers: long and strong, they'd do amazing things to her sensory nerves if they ever touched her skin.

He cleared his throat, forcing her to look up and lock gazes with him. A thoughtful expression tightened his face, darkened the fudge colour of his eyes to mud. So he wasn't happy with her.

'About this morning at the accident site…' He hesitated. 'When I saw that child lying there I got a shock and made a mistake. Sammy fell out of a tree once, broke his arm and got concussed. He was very lucky. For some reason this morning seemed like a rerun, only worse.'

Not about her, then. 'Sammy being Samuel, your son?' Another clue to this man's identity she'd overlooked that morning. But she *had* been more worried about Jason.

Brad's eyebrows flicked up, down. 'I take it that David has mentioned my family?'

'Only that you and your wife have been separated for about eighteen months and that Samuel is with his mother.' When Brad's lips tightened into a hard line she added, 'David only mentioned it after I quizzed him about you before you'd decided to come home to take over his medical practice while he sorts things out. I don't know all the details.'

'Is that why you gave me a bollocking over the phone?' His tone lifted in anger. 'What I chose to do was none of your business.'

Heat rushed into her cheeks. 'True, but half an hour before you rang I'd called in to see David and found him trying to wipe up the mug of coffee that he'd spilled over his clothes and the carpet. He was in a bit of a state, cross at his lack of control over a simple mug, embarrassed that I had to help him get out of his trousers.' She hesitated, reminded herself she had to work with this man, and added, 'I'm sorry I took it out on you.'

'It must've been difficult for you.'

'Only because David's stubbornly independent.' And because she'd often seen him sitting on the veranda of his big old house staring down the drive as though waiting for Brad to arrive. David had needed Brad desperately, and she'd told him. Rightly, or wrongly. Make that wrongly. She should've kept her mouth shut. On the other hand, it had worked and David was happier than he'd been in a long time.

'Isn't he just? Stubborn as an ox. And you were right that night. It is my place to be here for David. I owe him a lot.'

'I heard you lived with David and Mary as a teenager.'

He nodded. 'They rescued me from foster-care when I got into trouble with the law. David always listens to people, especially youngsters who don't have anyone on their side. I gave them merry hell at times, but they were always there for me from the day I met them.' Brad leaned back in his chair, tipped his head to stare up at the ceiling. 'I should've come the moment David told me about the Parkinson's, given him the time off to reassess his priorities. But I was caught between two people—David and my son.'

Not an easy choice. Why was he telling her this? Did he feel he had to justify his actions to her? 'Haven't Samuel and his mother moved to California?'

He winced. 'Yes.'

So, what had stopped him coming, then? Glancing at his stern face, she thought better of asking. But she couldn't imagine what it must've been like for Brad to have his son taken so far away. To only see him on rare occasions when he'd have been used to having Samuel in his life every day must've broken his heart. It was one thing not to be able to have a child, but to have one and lose him? That was far beyond her comprehension. She'd never feel complete again if it happened to her.

On the desk the phone buzzed discreetly. Grateful for the interruption, Erin slipped out the door, leaving Brad to answer it. Leaving Brad with a haunted look in his eyes.

Panic rose, threatened to engulf her. She could not share the clinic with this man. She'd go crazy trying to deal with all the emotions that whirled through her at the sight of him. A moment ago she'd wanted to hug away that haunted look. Imagine if she'd attempted to? He'd have been furious. How was she going to manage? One day at a time? Impossible. One minute at a time?

* * *

Brad watched Erin go as he slowly reached for the phone. What a motormouth he'd turned into all of a sudden, raving on about personal things to her, exposing himself to her scorn. *Which hadn't been forthcoming.* He'd grown to expect derision from Blenheim folk ever since his wayward youth spent here. The one time he'd talked to Erin on the phone she'd been so scathing in her criticism of him that he'd believed she was just another disgruntled Blenheimite, but she'd managed to make him think about how he was letting David down, made him realise it was time to move on from what Penelope had done.

The pain that had stabbed him when he'd talked about Sammy to Erin was ebbing. She still didn't know how he'd struggled to leave the apartment where he and Penelope had brought Sammy home as a four-day-old infant; where he'd taught his boy to play ball in the back yard; where he'd told him endless stories, attempting to get him to go to sleep. The apartment was crammed with sweet memories Brad hadn't been able to bring himself to leave. The rooms were filled with the sound of Sam's laughter. His childish drawings still adorned the walls of his bedroom and the kitchen. His rugby ball lay discarded by the back door, not needed in his new life.

The phone stopped ringing.

Brad spun around in his chair to stare out the window at the back of a brick wall beyond which rose the ugly sight of a supermarket.

'God, Sammy, I miss you so much. Sunday night phone calls are just not enough, buddy.' He needed to touch his boy, to hug him and talk with him. Hearing his excited chatter over the phone did not make up for not being able to see Sam's eyes grow as big as plates and his mouth curl up into a happy smile as he explained how he'd hit a run at baseball.

Baseball. A goddamned Yankee game. What was wrong with good old rugby? A game that Kiwis and Aussies loved? A man should be able to teach his boy the rudiments of a real bloke's game.

Someone knocked on his door, and Marilyn's face appeared tentatively around the edge. 'ED is on the line regarding Jason. Is there something wrong with your phone line? I put the call through here.'

'Try again, Marilyn. I'll get it this time.' He gave her a smile, the kind that usually got him most things he wanted. Except in Blenheim. Would it work with Erin? Would she fall for his charms? More likely she'd tell him to go take a flying leap off a very high cliff.

This time he took the call. 'Perano.'

'Roger Bailey, ED, Blenheim Hospital.'

'Roger, as in the best oarsman Otago Med School ever put up against Canterbury?' Brad hoped this was one man who'd accept him back in town without prejudice. Roger had loathed Penelope from the start, bringing tension between the two men.

'Didn't do us a lot of good, considering some of the useless dudes we had on that team. You still kicking a rugby ball around?'

'Not since I tore a ligament in my shoulder and decided I was getting too soft.' Not since my son was stolen from me.

'How are you anyway? I hear you're back to keep David out of trouble.'

'Only for a few months.' But even in the week since he'd arrived here, Brad had noticed some of the tension lining David's mouth easing, making him wonder how he'd be able to leave again.

'Right, about Jason Curtis.'

'Go on.' Brad sighed with relief. No mention of his ex-wife, then. The local gossip machine had probably put out an all-points bulletin about the state of Brad Perano's marriage before he'd even made the decision to move back home. Glad to have avoided the subject, Brad listened to everything Roger had to say about their young patient.

Roger filled him in quickly and efficiently. 'I'm flying Jason up to Starship Children's Hospital in Auckland on the medical emergency plane. I'm not happy about the head injury and we don't have a resident neurosurgeon here. I'm probably being over-cautious but better that way than thinking we can handle his problems and having it backfire on us.'

Brad hung up, and noted his computer informing him he had two patients waiting to be seen. 'Great, now *I'm* running late.' What had happened to the idea of coming in early and being very organised by the time the clinic opened for business?

He'd tell Erin about Jason later. Erin. The name suited her. Damn it. Why couldn't she be called Gertrude or Winifred? Then he'd be able to recall his austere great-aunts every time he looked at her, and forget the blinding passion that had rocked him earlier. Being squashed in that kennel-size shop, he'd felt dizzy with the scent of her.

Erin.

Damn it. He had to work with her. Like it or not. She could be another problem to add to an already overly long list of problems, starting with a town that he had to get back on side with.

Erin's only a problem if you let her be, squeaked a pesky little voice in his head.

Brad shoved the voice aside and went in search of his first patient. Nothing like focussing on someone else's problems to forget his own for a while.

Erin sat at the tiny table in the centre's kitchen and bit into her salad sandwich. Not exactly the most exciting lunch but it was all she'd had time to slap together after the way her morning had gone.

'I'd have thought you'd be munching on burgers and fries, getting all the carbs you can after your early morning ride.' Brad dropped onto a chair opposite her, threatening its flimsy legs with his weight.

'She would if I didn't nag her to be healthy.' David beat her to answering Brad as he walked in behind him.

Erin rolled her eyes at the man who'd been more like a father to her than her own had. She knew he was hoping Brad would buy him out of the practice. 'One of the drawbacks of working with David is that he thinks he can order me around.'

'He was always like that with me too.' Brad snagged a muffin out of the goodies basket David had brought in for all the staff as he officially handed over the last of his patients to Brad. 'By the way, David, I've got two young rascals to mow your lawns for you. They're going to cost you twenty bucks a fortnight, starting this afternoon.'

'That's a lot of money for two lads.'

'You've got a lot of lawn.'

'Those boys who wanted my bike? You're giving them a job?' Erin stared at Brad. 'Is that wise?'

'*You* told them you'd give them a job if you could. I just happened to think of one.'

David was looking from her to Brad and back again. 'Did you two meet before this morning?'

Erin stared at the remains of her sandwich and dropped it on the plate, pushed it aside. 'We bumped into each other at the shop and then again at Jason's accident just along the road.'

'Hardly surprising when you live next door to each other, I guess.' David studied his muffin as though seeing it for the first time.

'Neighbours?' Brad sounded shocked, and that hurt. Did he hate the idea? Or did he see some advantages?

Erin hadn't made her own mind up about the situation yet, but one thing was for sure: there was no changing it. She wasn't moving, and Brad had to stay with David while helping him out so they were stuck with each other living close by.

Brad was asking her, 'Which is your house?'

'The townhouse at the bottom of David's drive-way. Two years ago I came to Blenheim looking for a job and wanting to buy my own place. I went to an open home and David was there, trying to sell this wonderful brand-new home. We got talking and by the time I went back to my motel that night I had a house and a job. Amazing how things work out sometimes.' Those two pieces of good fortune had made her think the move to Blenheim was meant to be.

'Best thing you ever did, my girl. For me anyway.' David stood up. 'Anyone for coffee?'

'No, thanks.' Erin leaned over the back of her chair to dig inside the fridge for a can of soda she'd put there earlier. The snap of the tab was loud in the sudden silence.

Brad was watching her, a thoughtful expression clouding his face. 'Where did you move from?'

He was full of questions.

'I was of no fixed abode. An army brat who grew up and then joined the very service I'd hated all my childhood.' Always shifting from one base to the next, new schools and new kids to get on side with. The only constant had been Jonathon. For some bizarre reason, more often than not they found themselves living at the same base and going to the same school. He'd been her best friend who became her husband. The services had been the only life she'd known. She'd panicked when the time had come to choose a career and a town to live in. The services had been a safe option.

'So you left the army to do your nursing training?' Brad sounded genuinely interested.

'No, I took three years' leave when I turned twenty. Then once I'd qualified I transferred from the signals corps to the medical unit.' She got up and shoved a window open. Brad seemed to consume all the air, leaving none for her. 'It's hot in here,' she said lamely, then glanced at her watch. 'Oops, I've got a patient coming in for her hep. A shot. Lucky girl's off to Tanzania next month.'

At the door she stopped, remembering Katie Bryant. 'Brad, I've made an appointment for you to see Katie Bryant. She came in for her immunisation shots this morning. I tried to get her mother to stay on this morning but she already had another appointment at the dentist.'

Erin paused, thought about the unease she'd felt when she'd seen Katie. 'I would've talked to either of you first but you were both busy at the time. I think there's something wrong with Katie but I don't know what. Just a gut feeling. She's pale, underweight, sleeps a lot.'

'When's her mother bringing her back?' Brad asked, wariness edging his voice. The same caution she'd noted in Alison's voice when they'd talked about Katie.

'Wednesday morning. I tried to persuade her to bring Katie before then but with nothing specific to go on I didn't succeed.'

Brad turned to David. 'Are Katie and her mother related to Joey Bryant?'

'Wife and daughter.'

Brad's Adam's apple bobbed. 'Maybe you should see them.'

David caught Brad's eye. 'No. You've got to start somewhere and Joey's family is perfect.'

Brad stared at David for a long moment before turning to Erin and asking, 'Does the mother think there was anything out of the ordinary with her daughter?'

What was going on here? Something had just gone down between David and Brad that she couldn't understand. Erin focussed on the question Brad had asked. She'd think about the rest later. 'Not at all. Said it was nice that Katie had begun sleeping so well. Sleeping has always been a problem with her, driving her parents to despair at times.' She sipped her soda. 'I'm probably wasting everyone's time but I want to be sure.'

Erin Foley. Brad hadn't managed to dispel her image from his mind all day. Not even his trepidation about seeing Joey's wife had wiped his mind clear of the nurse. Which said a lot because he was as nervous as hell about talking to Alison. Maybe when Alison told Joey who their new GP was, their appointment would be cancelled. That would not be good for little Katie and more than anything Brad wanted to do what was best for his patients. Erin was concerned about the girl so he must see her.

Erin. His brain always switched back to her. When she'd arrived at the medical centre in such a damned hurry that morning and he'd seen that mass of shining black curls tumbling down her back, he'd have fallen flat on his face if he hadn't grabbed the filing cabinet. She was a knockout.

She'd flustered him, her laughter echoing through the building when she'd been with those children first thing. She certainly had a way with her that had made each one of them giggle and talk non-stop, forgetting about the needle about to stab their thigh. She'd make a great mother, if that was anything to go by.

An unbidden thought, an unwanted one, entered his head. Did she have a partner? David had said she lived alone, which surely meant no partner, no children? But a beautiful woman like Erin would never be completely single. There had to be a man somewhere in her life.

That idea made Brad's good mood evaporate in an instant. Which was plain silly. He did not want to get involved with any female. Been there, done the time. A fling might be all right but he wasn't having one with Erin Foley. *A bad idea in the circumstances.*

'Goodnight, Dr Perano,' Marilyn called from behind her desk.

He paused. 'What would it take to get you to

call me Brad?' Marilyn appeared to be in her late fifties, and seemed a stickler for protocol. So far she'd refused to budge on using his first name, but he was determined to win. Judging by the set of her jaw, it might take a while.

'I'm sizing you up, young man. Give me time.'

Did she know of him from the past? He didn't recall her at all, but the stories about him might have coloured her perception of him even before they'd met.

'Young man?' Brad muttered. 'I'm thirty-four.'

'And I'm sixty-four, so be patient.' She stood and pushed her chair under her desk, then leaned down to retrieve her handbag from the floor. Then she looked him in the eye. 'Just be good to our David and you'll have me calling you any damned thing you like.'

So he was on notice from the office staff. But the fact that David's staff cared so much for the older man actually made Brad hum as he opened the door to the car park. He might've been slow in getting here but others had stepped up to the mark. Guilt caught him. David had shown no censure towards him. Which only said how big-hearted the man was and how much further indebted *he* had become.

Outside David called to him from beside his car. 'You on your way home, too? Want me to pick up anything from the supermarket?'

'No, I've got all I need to cook tonight's dinner.' Brad scratched his chin thoughtfully. 'So Erin lives down the bottom of our drive. That's kind of handy for you.'

'Perfect situation.' David raised pale blue eyes to him. 'Don't tell me you're bothered by it? Why would you be?'

Because she'd be too close to him. There'd be no getting away from her. It was one thing that they'd be working together. He could probably manage to keep her at arm's length here, but to have her practically living on his doorstep meant he'd never have peace of mind. He slapped his hands on his hips and stared across at David, suddenly cross. 'I don't like it.'

'Erin's been very helpful and always there if I've needed anything.' David talked as though he hadn't seen Brad's angst, but Brad knew better. David missed nothing, and now his eyes twinkled suspiciously. 'I think you two will get along very well.'

'You are so wrong.' They'd light up like flames with petrol added. Something indefinable and hot already sat between them, something he wasn't prepared to explore.

'Give her a chance. Get to know her. You'll like her.'

I already like her. A lot. Too much. But bitter experience had taught him people weren't always what they first seemed to be. 'You could be wrong.'

'Bradley, you give her a chance. I'll not have you upsetting the cosy set-up we've got at work or anywhere else.'

David only called him Bradley when he wanted to make a point, but that didn't stop Brad arguing. 'It's not wise to socialise with staff.'

David chuckled. 'You can't expect me to agree with that. Not when my Mary was a nurse on my surgical ward when I was an intern.'

'There are always exceptions.' Was the old boy matchmaking?

How much worse could this get?

CHAPTER THREE

'WHAT a day I've had, Lucky.' Erin chattered to her cat as she drove carefully through the streets towards home. 'First day back and already I feel like my holiday is so long ago it didn't happen.'

Lucky was unusually silent, sitting in the cage staring straight ahead, ignoring Erin entirely.

'Come on, stop sulking. It's not as though I left you incarcerated in some dire cat hostel with no one to care for you. I know for a fact you've been pampered beyond your wildest dreams.' The fees had been horrendous, but well worth it. The Paws Cattery came highly recommended.

'We've got a new neighbour.' Her mouth turned up into a reluctant smile. 'He's gorgeous.' An image of Brad on his Harley-Davidson made her mouth water. She'd been putting drugs away in the clinic's fridge when the bike had roared to life outside. Discreetly nudging aside the curtain a tad, she'd studied the man who'd had her heart rate rising and falling alarmingly throughout the day. The Harley belonged with him, balanced perfectly between those muscular thighs, adding to his sexiness. Brad intrigued her, confused her, and had her wondering what it would be like to get to know him.

To have an affair with him? The steering-wheel flicked sideways. She straightened the car, her heart pounding in her throat. Just thinking about Brad was dangerous.

'Definitely no affair,' she reassured Lucky. Brad would be used to experienced women, not someone who'd only ever known one man intimately. Anyway, she liked her life where no man told her how to live, where to work, when to cook dinner.

But an affair might get this sizzling sensation out of her blood so her life could return to the peaceful state it had been in when she'd woken up that morning. But, no, it wasn't going to happen. Affairs always ended with bad feelings on at least one side, which would not bode well for working with Brad afterwards. So she lied to the cat. 'Brad's not my type, Lucks. Don't you go schmoozing up to him, either.'

Lucky continued staring ahead, rocking slightly as Erin turned into her drive.

'You just remember you're on my side.' She really, really wished Brad could go and live somewhere else. But that also wasn't going to happen. David needed him so she couldn't deprive David of the man he considered his son.

The garage door lifted and Erin nosed the car inside. 'Home, sweet home, Lucky. Let's see if some of your favourite gourmet tuna feast will make you love me again.'

Out of her cage, Lucky arched her back and stared around. Erin sighed and picked up laden grocery bags. In the kitchen she dumped the bags on the bench and switched the oven on to heat up a ready-made pasta bake. Turning, she gasped. 'What the—?'

Drawers from the dresser were on the floor, their contents spilled out over the floor. Apprehension filled her. Had she been burgled? She glanced around warily. Someone had certainly been in here. She'd locked up before she'd left for work that morning. Hadn't she? She had been in a rush. Maybe she hadn't checked all the locks.

What if the thief's still here? Her heart rose in her throat. Reaching a shaking hand into the utensil drawer, she removed the rolling pin.

'Lucky?' The cat stood in the centre of the kitchen, her back still arched, her eyes wild. 'Are we alone? Can you hear anyone moving around?'

Lucky's head flicked from side to side. Not a lot to go on. Erin sucked a breath. She'd done self-defence training in the army, and come up against some big, stroppy men in the process. A burglar couldn't get the better of her.

Raising the rolling pin, she did a quick, thorough search of her home. No one hid behind the doors or in the wardrobes. Upstairs in her bedroom drawers had been emptied over the bed, and some small change had gone, but as far as she could make out that was all that was missing. Kids?

Down in her laundry the door that led out into the garden wide was open. Closer inspection showed it had been jemmied so now it wouldn't shut properly.

Feeling more confident, Erin quickly walked around the outside but found no trace of her burglar. Glancing across to the trees that bordered onto her section from David's place, she made to go and search there, hesitated. Maybe not a wise idea. The area around those trees looked darker than usual.

Returning inside, she picked up the phone and dialled the cop who lived in the adjoining town-house. No reply. Next she tried David's number. She didn't want him to coming racing down here but he might've noticed someone loitering.

'David Taylor's house. Can I help you?' That disturbingly sexy voice rolled down the line at her.

Of course Brad would answer. How silly of her not to think of that.

His voice snapped into her musings. 'Hello? Any one there?'

'Yes, It's Erin.' Then added, 'Erin Foley.'

'Yes, I think I know who Erin is. Super nurse and crazy cyclist.'

'Why crazy cyclist?'

'Anyone who prefers to pedal than use a motor has to be crazy.'

So he wasn't an exercise freak. Again the image of Brad on his Harley rose before her eyes.

'Erin? I find one-sided phone calls rather awkward.'

She shook her head. 'Sorry. Is David there? I wondered if he'd seen anyone hanging around the back of my house. Or maybe in his front garden.'

'Why? Has something happened? Are you all right?'

'I'm fine. But my house has been broken into.'

'Don't go outside. Lock all the doors. I'm on my way.'

'Too late, I've already checked out there.' But her words fell into a void as Brad banged down the phone at his end. She pushed redial. She didn't want that Goliath in her house. His presence would make it feel claustrophobic. She wouldn't know what to say to him. 'Answer the phone.'

He didn't.

He thumped the back door repeatedly, calling out, 'Erin, it's me, Brad. Open up.' He did not want to be here, about to walk into her home. Like walking into the lioness's den. But he couldn't ignore the fact Erin might be in trouble.

'It's not locked,' he heard her call. His top teeth ground across the bottom ones. Hadn't he told her to lock up?

The door swung open, revealing Erin with her arms full of a grey tabby. 'Come in.'

'You should've checked it was me before you opened the door,' he growled. His hands gripped his hips, his chest rising and falling after his frantic run down here.

'Your voice is very distinctive.' Her face coloured as she stepped back, holding the door wide. 'Anyway, the lock is broken.'

His voice distinctive? How? 'I'll take a look at it.'

'Thanks. I've already looked around outside. No one was hiding behind the shrubs.'

'You did what?' His heart stuttered. 'What if your burglar had been out there? You could've been attacked.'

'I'll have you know I'm very well trained in

self-defence.' But there was a sheepish look in those startlingly blue eyes.

'I'm sure you are.' But he didn't like the idea someone might've hurt her. Even more, he didn't like it that he cared a lot about what happened to her. He stepped inside and pushed the door closed behind him, leaning back against it. Why her sheepish look?

'Come through. Did you ask David if he'd seen anyone hanging around?' She shrugged at him as though she didn't care if he followed her or not.

Brad didn't believe that nonchalance. It sounded forced. His estimation of her rose higher. She was one brave woman. He placed his hand on her shoulder, forcing her to turn around and meet his gaze full on. A hint of worry lurked in the deep blue shadows. 'Want me to take a look through your house?'

The cat tensed in her arms, and Erin ran a soothing hand down its back. 'I already did. The drawers in the kitchen dresser and my bedroom have been rifled but nothing else seems to have been touched.'

'Then you're fortunate.' Relief swamped him.

At least she was safe. He dropped his hand, but not before her heat radiated up his arm, sending jolts of yearning through his body.

'I guess, but it does annoy me, someone breaking in. Whoever it was took a few dollars but that seems to be all.' Her tongue slid across her bottom lip.

Brad dragged a hand over his head, trying to ignore her sweet mouth and the need to kiss it brought on by her action. Stepping back, he bumped up against the door again. 'I'll see what's needed to repair your door.'

'I've got some tools in the garage if you require them. Help yourself.'

'Maybe you should call the police.'

Erin told him, 'My neighbour's a cop but he's not home yet. I'll call the watch house later.'

'Okay.' Brad left her and went to poke around in her minimal tool collection for a hammer and nails. 'This'll help secure the door for now but tomorrow I'll get a new lock and install it,' he told her as he passed the kitchen again.

'Thank you, but that won't be necessary. I'll phone the locksmith in the morning.'

He had a sudden suspicion. 'Any idea what time this happened?'

She shook her head, sending her shiny black hair swirling around her shoulders. 'I only got home a few minutes ago.'

'Cain and Tony.' He'd bet his Harley on them being the culprits.

'Who?'

'The two boys from this morning. I had them come around and meet David before they mow his lawns next weekend. I'm trying to teach them that they have to earn money for the things they want in life. Which I think you mentioned to them quite forcefully.' It had been her comments that had made him think about ways to help the boys.

'There's quite a leap from walking off with an abandoned bike to being guilty of breaking and entering.' Amusement lit up her eyes.

'You might be right.' But the more he thought about it the more certain he was he'd found the culprits. 'Will you give me a chance to talk to them before you talk to the cops?'

She folded her arms under her breasts. His

mouth dried, and he had to struggle to hear her through the pounding in his ears.

'How long have you known those boys?'

'Since this morning.' *Most of my life. They are me at that age.* 'I've found out about their backgrounds. Not good. I'd like to help them if I can.' *Like David and Mary did for me.*

Her gaze was disconcerting. As was her next question. 'You sure you know what you're doing?'

'Yes.' He wouldn't plead for her to understand him. Neither would he divulge his history, if she didn't already know it, in order to win some slack for the boys. She had to accept his opinion.

'Okay.'

'That's it? No conditions? No questions? You'll let me talk to them first?' She'd surprised him. Deflated him, really. He sucked a breath, added belatedly, 'Thanks.'

She nodded. 'I'll make some coffee while you're fixing that door.'

'I'd prefer a beer.' Brad slipped into the laundry and tackled the broken lock.

Either the kettle was slow or he was fast because soon he was standing in her kitchen, watching her put her groceries away. The cat strolled across and used his boots to sharpen its claws. Unperturbed, he hunkered down and rubbed the back of its neck with his forefinger. 'What's the moggy's name?'

'Lucky. Lucky I found her at the SPCA.'

'So you're into looking out for strays, too.' Cats. Boys. They all needed love and understanding.

Looking up at Erin, his chest tightened. Her gaze was fixed on his finger stroking the cat. A light flush coloured her cheeks, sending his imagination running riot. It wasn't hard to envisage caressing her skin. Hell, it seemed they only had to be together for a few moments and the fireworks started.

He stood, breaking the contact with Lucky and hopefully shifting Erin's intense stare from him. But her head came up and she locked gazes with him. A hot, intense gaze that left him breathless. 'Erin?'

She jerked her head sideways, broke the grip of that look. Opening the fridge, she dug out a beer, handed it over, careful not to touch his outstretched fingers.

He took a swig of the cold nectar, swallowed

around the lump in his throat. Sucked in a great lungful of air. And tried to concentrate on looking around the kitchen with its modern appliances. 'Very classy kitchen. I've never been inside these townhouses.' Because he hadn't been here for so long.

'Take a look around. The architect did an amazing job. I fell in love with the high ceilings and big windows that make the place feel larger than it is.'

'I'll take a look some other time.' As if he intended coming back. Erin's place had to be out of bounds if he was going to maintain some semblance of control.

But he did look through to the dining room. Spartan, with only a table and two chairs. No sideboards, no casual chairs, no flowers. Sterile. Somehow he'd have picked Erin for a homemaker with beautiful things around her.

He almost leapt in the air when she spoke right behind him. 'Old habits die hard.'

Spinning around, he sucked a breath, she was so close. If he leaned forward he could effortlessly kiss those full lips. He leaned back. 'What old habits?'

'The less stuff you have the easier it is to pack when you get transferred, and sometimes transfers happened more often than haircuts.' Thankfully she moved back to the kitchen bench, taking her floral scent with her. Taking temptation out of the way.

'To think that my place in Adelaide is chock-full of everything from a computer to a Ford Mustang.' His laugh sounded hollow in the quiet house.

She smiled over her shoulder at him. 'A Mustang? Really?'

'I'm restoring it. It's been a long job so far.' He couldn't take his eyes off her as she poured the boiling water over the grounds, pressed the plunger, poured the coffee into a large mug. He sucked in every inch of skin to avoid contact when she moved past him with her drink, but still her arm brushed against his, and the coffee slopped in the mug.

'Sorry,' he muttered.

The mug banged on the glass-topped table in the lounge as she put it down. Then she straightened, and Brad's heart slammed against his ribs. She was simply beautiful. He wished he had the strength to tell his heart to go take a flying leap instead of thumping so hard the whole street must be able to hear it.

Everything else stopped at that instant. Neither of them breathed. Outside the world had gone quiet, like that pregnant moment before an earthquake struck. The only sound was the pounding in his chest. Thump. Thump. Thump.

Erin shifted, and again he had to grab a lungful of air as he fought the overwhelming urge to kiss her. Those full lips held him enthralled. His body bent towards her without him having any conscious thought. And Erin leaned towards him. Her eyes were wide, the blue so dark it was like looking at a night sky without the stars. Her breath touched his cheek, sending tendrils of desire winding through him.

Lifting his head, he glanced over her shoulder, and blinked. Startled, he straightened up from her, turned to study the room. Again minimally furnished with two armchairs, the coffee table and a small bookcase. Three photographs were neatly arranged on top of the bookcase. Photos of Erin and a man. Happy photos. Cuddling, smiling poses.

Brad stepped away from Erin. He'd nearly kissed her. Damn it, she'd have let him, too. His hands clenched at his sides. What kind of woman did that? Kissed a virtual stranger when she already had a man in her life?

But he already knew the answer. The kind of woman his ex-wife had been. A woman on the make, clawing her way out of a poverty-stricken background, willing to use anyone, anything, on her way to wealth and comfort. Why had Erin brought him in here when she had to know he'd see those photos? Did she have an agenda and forgot about the pictures?

Right now her eyes were wide, her mouth a round O. When he'd stepped back she'd whipped around to see what had startled him. Her shoulders had drooped and she sank onto one of the chairs, gripping her hands in her lap. She whispered, 'I can explain.'

'I'm sure you can.' But he didn't want to hear excuses or lies made up to make her look better.

He knew that storyline, had lost his son because of it. He turned for the door, needing to put as much space between them as possible. He couldn't believe he'd been about to make the same mistake again. Was he so inherently flawed that he chose women who didn't know how to remain faithful to one man?

'That man in the photos is Jonathon, my husband.' Her voice faltered. 'My late husband.'

Brad froze, his retreat halted. Her husband had died? And he'd reacted without thinking there was any other explanation, tarring this woman with the same selfish characteristics as Penelope. Turning, he was surprised to find Erin watching him, sadness mixed with hurt in her eyes.

He swore under his breath. Damn, but he was stupid. Would he never learn that not everyone was out to take what they could from him? Not every female he was attracted to would cheat on him. Worse, now he'd made such a monumental faux pas, how would he and Erin get past it? His head ached with all the questions buzzing around inside.

Quietly she added, 'Jonathon died in an accident

more than two years ago. I guess I should've put the photos away by now.' Her shoulders lifted, rolled, drooped again. 'I've never been able to bring myself to do it.'

Two years ago she'd moved to Blenheim. To get away from the memories? His fingers dug into his hips. 'I'm so sorry for jumping to the wrong conclusion. I really am.'

The hurt rolled across her face, causing guilt to cramp his stomach. He'd do anything to be able to retract his words. He didn't like her thinking badly of him. He needed to think before reacting. Not his strong point.

She asked, 'Do you always see the worst in people?'

'I try not to.' He looked at her, feeling his facial muscles tighten with his need for her to believe him. 'But sometimes other things, other influences, get in the way and I manage to put both my great big feet into my mouth.'

'I loved my husband. Still have feelings for him.' She picked up her coffee and gazed deep inside the mug.

Brad looked at the photos again. Looked properly without the clouded vision of anger at being taken for a fool. A tinge of something foreign tugged at him. Envy? For such happiness displayed between Erin and her husband?

How could he envy a dead guy? Why would he when he had no intention of getting close to Erin? *You nearly kissed her. Is that not getting close?*

Brad gasped. 'I think I'd better go.'

'You haven't drunk your beer,' she murmured.

'I'll take it with me.' He doubted she really wanted him to stay while he finished it. Unless she was afraid to be left alone after the break-in. 'You don't have a flatmate?'

'No. After spending years in the army I didn't want anyone sharing my bathroom.'

'I can understand that.' He'd always liked his own space. 'I take it you don't have any children.'

'No.' Pain squeezed her eyes narrow, her generous mouth flat.

'Have I done it again? Put my huge foot where my mouth is supposed to be?'

Her voice was a whisper, so low he strained to hear her words. But the sadness was apparent in the way her body sagged into the chair. Her eyes focussed on a photo of herself with her husband. 'We were trying. The whole IVF thing. But it wasn't working. Seems I can't have babies.'

Definitely both feet in his mouth. What did he say to that? 'Erin.' Brad shook his head. 'You must think I'm a totally uncaring man with my questions. I hope you forgive me.' He'd certainly get the prize for being the insensitive idiot of the year. But people asked these questions every day and usually got away with them. And he really did want to know more about Erin.

Because he had to work with her. Of course. So he'd be asking all the clinic staff the same things?

'It's okay. Now you know. But don't feel sorry for me. I've made a great life for myself. This place and my job are my life, my focus now.' She drained her mug and fixed a big smile on her face that was as false as blue moons. 'I don't know why I'm telling you these things. Maybe because of that near kiss. I don't know what came over me.' Her cheeks coloured in a heart-tearing way. 'I don't usually get involved with men in case I find myself attracted to a man whose dream is to have six kids.'

A truckload of pain laced her words, soured that bright, forced smile. He felt for her, understood that pain completely. But all he said was, 'I can imagine that could be tricky.'

She stood up. 'I'll see you at work tomorrow.'

He suspected she was already regretting talking to him. Unable to stop himself, he crossed to lay a gentle kiss on her warm cheek. 'Goodnight, Erin.'

For the second time that day he thought she'd make a wonderful mother. Damn it, with someone like Erin as Samuel's mother, life would be so much better.

Her perfume, lightly floral, followed him outside, stayed with him as he strode up the drive to David's house.

What about an affair to get her out of your blood? The situation was perfect. Erin couldn't have kids; he didn't do permanent relationships. If they stuck to what simmered between them then neither would get hurt.

Except it had been obvious in Erin's wobbly voice, in her sad eyes, in the false smile, that she wasn't that kind of girl. Deep down she wanted a man in her life.

Tugging the Harley key out of his back pocket, Brad headed for the garage. His bike throbbed between his thighs, the roar of the engine breaking through the quiet evening. The warm air caressed his arms as he roared away from Bexley Road and the problem of Erin Foley.

What a blabbermouth she'd turned into. Erin turned the oven off and headed upstairs to bed. Her appetite had disappeared about the time she'd nearly fallen into Brad's arms. Even now she felt the anticipation of that kiss, felt the sizzle in her veins. If not for those photos she'd now know what it was like to be kissed by Bradley Perano.

She heard the motorbike roar past her house. 'So our doctor likes to ride the roads at night,' she muttered, a feeling of wickedness enveloping her. What would it be like to ride on the back of his bike? Forget the bike. Winding her arms around Brad would be the excitement.

Flicking the bedcovers back, Erin earned a hiss

from Lucky, who had been turning circles on the bed, readying for a good night's sleep.

'Don't you hiss at me, you schmoozer. Didn't I specifically tell you not to cuddle up to Brad?' But who was she to complain about being beguiled by the man when she'd been yearning for his fingers to soothe her hot skin, not the cat's fur. The wicked feeling increased as images of Brad slid through her mind. Sliding between her cool sheets only brought more pictures, graphic ones of that muscular body, naked, stretched out beside her, in this bed.

Even with the windows open the room was warm, stifling. Erin's hand hovered over the bedside light switch. Did she want to turn it off and give her mind free rein in the dark to conjure up more images of Brad? No, better to read for a while, and try putting him out of her mind.

Reaching for her book on the bedside table, another of Jonathon caught her attention. 'I'm sorry, Jonathon. I shouldn't be having these thoughts about another man. It's not right, I know, but I can't help myself.'

Staring at her late husband's beautiful face, his

wide smile seemed to be just for her. His eyes looked right through to her heart. Understanding her? Forgiving her? Her hand shook. Of course he'd want her to move on and be happy.

But she didn't deserve happiness. Not when it was her fault he'd died. 'I'm so sorry,' Erin whispered. 'I don't need a baby as much as I need you back in my life.'

It was the zillionth apology, and it felt no better than any of the others. The deep pain that she'd carried all this time had lightened, not disappeared. Tonight her emotions were brighter, sharper. Because of her ridiculous attraction to a virtual stranger?

She stared into the face of the only man she'd loved. They'd met when they were both seven, their families having been transferred to Papakura Military Camp at the same time. They'd been best friends ever since Jonathon had kicked a boy in the shins for calling Erin a skinny weasel. That friendship had grown as they'd got older, eventually becoming lovers.

Now she wondered about that love. It had held none of the passion she'd felt around Brad today.

Passion that heated her blood, warmed her muscles and tightened her stomach. 'Get over it. This is lust, pure and simple. Love is what Jonathon and I had.'

Lucky snuggled closer, and Erin's free hand stroked her. 'Yes, and you're my first ever pet.' The cat was the closest she would come to having a child. Would Jonathon have married her if he'd known about her infertility?

As she put the photo back her heart again crunched with pain. If she hadn't been so driven to conceive a baby Jonathon wouldn't have been driving back in the middle of the night, exhausted from tough military exercises. 'I did love you so much.'

She snapped the light off and shuffled down the bed. 'What? I *did* love you?' Oh, no. She'd meant she still loved him. She couldn't have stopped loving him because she'd met a man who'd made her come alive. 'Maybe I've been moving on without realising, slowly letting go of Jonathon.'

That wasn't possible. That spelled disloyalty.

Tears welled up, spilled down her cheeks. Within minutes her pillow was drenched.

CHAPTER FOUR

'HAVE you called a locksmith yet?' Brad asked Erin as she charged through the clinic first thing the next morning, a large, covered plate balanced in one hand.

'He's there as we speak,' she told him as she pushed past in the hallway, followed by a petite woman with a big smile.

Brad's gaze followed Erin. 'Good. I didn't like the idea of that door not being locked properly last night.'

'Believe me, that didn't keep me awake,' she called over her shoulder as she disappeared into the kitchen.

'But something did if we're getting cake this morning,' said the woman now standing beside him.

'Cake?'

'Standard practice if Erin's not sleeping very

well. She gets up and bakes, and we're the winners.' The woman put out her hand. 'Annie Johnston, GP. I work about thirty hours a week here.'

'Pleased to be working with you,' Brad said, then asked, 'You're not a local?'

'No. My husband works in the wine industry and we moved here five years ago.' Annie sniffed the air like a spaniel. 'What flavour?' she asked as Erin came back towards them.

'Passion fruit and vanilla layer cake.' Deep shadows darkened the skin under Erin's eyes, and her cheeks had lost their usual high colour.

Had she lain awake worrying about her break-in? Hopefully his news would help dispel any further worry on that score. 'I paid a visit to those two boys this morning. They admit to breaking in and stealing your money.'

'Do I get it back?'

'Long gone. So I've suggested they mow your lawns too, for the next month. If that's all right with you.'

She nodded, not looking at him. 'I like the idea. Hopefully they'll learn something from this and not go helping themselves to other people's things any more.'

'They're fairly harmless. I think it was more a cry for help.' Another thought occurred to him. Had that near kiss kept Erin up?

Annie stared at Erin. 'What's this? You had a break-in? Why didn't you phone Rick?'

'No need. I called David in case he'd noticed anyone lurking around and Brad answered.' A cheeky smile lifted her mouth momentarily. 'He does a good knight in shining armour.'

Brad blinked. 'I don't think so.' But he had rushed down to her place as though she'd been about to be murdered by some depraved maniac.

'Truthfully? I was glad you came. Thanks for temporarily sorting out the lock and checking everything out.'

'Your lock wasn't properly fixed?' Annie asked. 'Why didn't you come around and sleep at our place? No wonder you look so peaky.'

'Thanks a million,' Erin snapped. 'I was perfectly fine at home. I'll put the kettle on as I go past the kitchen.'

'I'll have mine in my office,' Brad muttered.

'I need to familiarise myself with my patient list for the day. I don't like any nasty surprises.' He needed to know if any patients were likely to give him grief over the past. Being prepared, having the right words sorted beforehand, made facing them a little bit easier.

'You're looking after David's patients, right?' Annie asked.

'Mostly,' Brad replied. 'Why?'

'I believe David has called most of them to explain that you'll be seeing them for the next few months. No one seemed at all fazed by the change.'

Brad's eyebrows rose. 'Is that so?' Obviously Annie didn't know he'd left under a cloud, deserted his mates without a backward glance, let them think he'd gone to jail, not to med school.

Just then the front door burst open and a man about Brad's age escorted in a very pregnant young woman clutching a bucket to her stomach. He demanded, 'Is Dr Taylor here yet? Lizzie's been throwing up all night.'

Erin materialised from somewhere behind him.

'He's on leave, Colin. Dr Perano's seeing his patients.'

Colin's head jerked around. 'Brad Perano? It is, too. Haven't seen you around for a long while. I'm surprised you came back to Blenheim.'

Brad felt the connection of those curious eyes, and surprised there was no hostility said, 'It's been a while since I was last here.'

'You fooled the lot of us when you went to Otago University. Thought we'd be visiting you in another place.' Colin winked, then turned to the woman on his arm. 'Lizzie's right crook. Must be something she ate but we're a bit worried about the baby, aren't we, love?'

Lizzie nodded.

Brad hadn't recognised her at first. She'd been about sixteen and as thin as a rake when they'd all knocked around together. Probably was still slim without the baby growing inside her. 'Are you happy if I examine you, Lizzie? Colin?'

'As long as your doctoring is better than your driving used to be, I guess we don't mind seeing you instead of Doc Taylor.' Colin gently steered Lizzie along the hall to Brad's office.

Brad shook his head in bemusement. 'Guess that's a yes, then.'

Erin stood in the middle of the room, staring at him, and Brad found himself explaining.

'He's referring to the time I, ah…borrowed David's car and, well…crashed it. Colin was with me.' Honesty made him add as he absently rubbed the scar on his chin, 'Because I coerced him into going with me. We never told the cops that. I said I was on my own.'

Erin's eyebrows disappeared somewhere over the top of her head. 'Very noble.'

'I thought so at the time.' Brad stomped down to his room, trying to ignore the niggle of shame Erin had caused to slide through him. It was hard enough dealing with the people who knew about his past, let alone introducing Erin to it all. He wanted her to think the best of him, to accept him for the man he'd become.

Entering his office, he found Colin and Lizzie staring at Samuel's photo on the desk.

Colin glanced up, tapped the photo with his finger. 'Heard you had a wee lad. This him?'

'Yes.' Brad waited for the smart-aleck comments to flow.

But all Colin said was, 'He doesn't look at all like you.' He settled Lizzie on to a chair. 'We're having a boy. Can't wait for him to pop out. It's going to be awesome. When they're all a bit older your boy could babysit mine.'

That was how it was all supposed to work in a perfect world. 'Samuel lives in America with Penelope.' And the familiar pain lanced him, cutting into his gut, tearing at his heart. His eyes sought the photo, his gaze latching onto his beautiful son. Would this pain, this yearning, ever abate? Or was he doomed to suffer for the rest of his life?

For the first time since she'd arrived Lizzie spoke. 'Brad, I'm so sorry. That must be hard to cope with. I wasn't surprised to hear Penelope had left you. She was always too restless to stay in one place, with one man for ever, but she should never have taken your boy away from you.'

How damned true. But how could he have prevented her? In the courts he hadn't had a leg to stand on. He'd had to back down or risk never even talking to Sammy again. 'Thanks, Lizzie.'

It was the best he could manage around the lump in the back of his throat. At least neither of these two had laughed at him for the events that had overtaken his life. 'Thanks, guys. Now, let's see why you've been vomiting all night, Lizzie.'

Lizzie's was the first case of food poisoning, but many followed. Erin couldn't remember ever being so busy at the medical centre. The days flew past. The health department put the outbreak down to poorly cooked chicken kebabs sold at a local diner. At times it seemed half the town had eaten the kebabs. Patients had been traipsing in ever since, meaning all the staff had put in longer hours than usual.

Being so hectic meant there was less time for Erin to dwell on Brad and his reaction to Colin and Lizzie. It had been like Brad was afraid they'd refuse to be treated by him, or start talking about him as though he'd been a monster when he'd lived here before. Sure, he'd stolen a car, but David and Mary had taken care of that escapade and Erin thought they'd probably saved Brad from furthering his criminal life. Not that she could really state that with certainty. Had he done other bad things? Was that why he didn't expect to be accepted here?

He had fitted into the routine at the centre even if he was often wary of his patients. Now she wondered how they'd been managing so long with David functioning at half his normal pace. In fact, David's condition seemed to be deteriorating, almost as though he was letting go his tenacious hold on the Parkinson's now that Brad had arrived to relieve him of his medical duties. What would they all do if Brad didn't fall into line with David's idea of the arrangement becoming permanent so that David could bow out completely?

'Daydreaming in the storeroom?' Brad broke through her questions.

Erin dropped the syringe she'd been holding. 'Don't creep up on me like that.' *And stop sucking up all the air in here.*

'Did Katie Bryant's latest results come through?'

'I left a note in your tray. Essentially Katie's doing fine. The transfusion worked and her hae-moglobin is now a healthy one hundred and one.'

Brad had taken one look at Katie on Wednesday

and immediately admitted her to hospital with anaemia due to dangerously low iron levels. He said, 'That's a relief. Have they found the cause of the iron loss?'

'The nurse told me the paediatrician believes it's dietary but the investigation is ongoing to find the reason behind that. You're to call the paediatrician at your leisure.' Erin cranked up a tired smile.

'His words?' Brad's eyebrows rose in that endearing manner she'd already come to love.

No, come to like, not love. Flustered, she nodded and turned away to fold up the laundry.

Brad didn't take the hint. 'You've got good instincts with your patients. If not for you things could've turned out a lot worse for Katie. If she'd had a fall and bled profusely, she mightn't have survived.'

Warmth stole over Erin at his compliment. 'Thanks. I just don't understand how her mum didn't notice anything.'

'The onset of anaemia was probably gradual so Alison wouldn't have noticed anything going wrong.' Brad then asked, 'Can you take some bloods for me?'

'Sure. Who's the patient?'

'Judge Marshall. I haven't marked the form urgent but can you get on to the lab after a reasonable length of time to chase up the results?'

'Give me the hard jobs, why don't you?' She smiled to take the sting out of her words. Ringing and asking for results didn't always go down well with the lab staff, especially this week when they also were snowed under with the dodgy chicken crisis.

'I think mine might take that dubious honour when we get those results.' Brad handed her the form, releasing it quickly. Worried she might inadvertently touch him?

Erin read the list of tests he'd asked for, then further down the page his comments. 'Bence Jones protein, ESR, CBC. You're wondering about multiple myeloma. Poor Judge Marshall.'

'He had a raised ESR last month and some intermittent pain in his legs and back, which has increased.'

'You think that's bone pain?'

'Unfortunately, yes.'

Sadness enveloped Erin. 'You don't know him

but he's a lovely man, always cheerful and talk-
ative when he comes in here for his regular check-
ups. Not at all snooty like some judges I've met.'

Brad leaned against the wall. 'You're wrong. I
knew him well when I was a teenager. Came up
before him more than once.'

'You did?' Guess that put paid to her theory that
the car 'borrowing' had been a one-off event. Why
did he keep telling her things like this? Trying to
get there before any rumours she might hear?

Brad escorted Henry Marshall into her room,
then stayed while she prepared to take the blood
samples.

The judge chatted easily. 'So, Bradley, I bet
David's pleased you're back, eh? He's been lonely
since Mary passed on. Are you staying in the big
house?'

'In the flat attached out the back. But I spend
a lot of time with David, sharing meals, watching TV.' Brad leaned against the wall as though
he didn't have another patient out in the waiting
room. Which Erin knew he did.

The older man continued. 'You've done well for
yourself. David's right proud of you, laddie. He's

always telling us at the club about your work in Adelaide.'

'Hey, laddie, I think we've got a new name for you.' Erin grinned at Brad's discomfort, and received a scowl for her trouble. Ignoring him, she turned to their patient. 'I hear you've finally retired, Mr Marshall.'

'Last month, in fact. I had intended finishing up last year but one of my partners had a heart attack so I agreed to stay on for a while. I'm planning a trip to Europe with the wife.' Then he seemed to remember why he was there and his face caved in. 'If we make it.'

Brad straightened up. 'Let's take one step at a time, Judge, before making decisions about anything.'

'Good advice.' The judge changed the subject. 'I remember when this man was all long legs and arms, and not a muscle in sight. Grew up all right, though.'

Erin chanced a glance at Brad and had to admit that the sight was stupendous. She took a deep breath to steady the needle in her hand.

'Think I've got another patient waiting.' Brad disappeared out the door.

Henry chuckled. 'Yes, he was the lad mothers warned their daughters to stay clear of.'

'Which only worked in my favour.' Brad briefly poked his head back around the door.

'I'm sure it did.' Henry winked at Erin as she changed a full tube for an empty one. 'Young lady, I hope your mother's nearby to warn you. Bradley still looks like he could be a handful for an attractive girl like you.'

Erin gawped at her patient. 'My parents live in Australia.' She couldn't think of anything else to say.

'Then I'm warning you.'

'Are you serious?' She looked directly at the judge and relaxed. His eyes sparkled with laughter. 'Not that I intend having anything to do with Brad outside work.' The judge was a cheeky old man and she'd love to box his ears.

David, who'd done a few hours each day to help out with the crisis, stood up and started to clear the table of empty chip packets and dirty glasses.

All the staff were crowded into the small kitchen area, enjoying a quiet drink. Brad had put on some wine and beer, along with nibbles, as a way to wind down after the busy week they'd had.

Erin stretched her legs under the table. 'Leave those. I'll clean up before I go.'

'Don't mind if I do. I'm a bit tired tonight.' David looked across at Brad. 'I'll see you later.'

Brad rolled his beer bottle between his hands. 'I won't be too long. I'm waiting on a call from the hospital and then I'll be heading home. What do you want for dinner?'

'Don't worry about cooking for me. I'll have an egg on toast.'

Marilyn pushed up from her chair. 'I'll be off too. My sister's coming over.'

Erin sighed. 'Thank heavens for weekends.' Now everyone had started packing up. 'I guess we're done here, then.' She wasn't going to be the last one left with Brad.

'Stay and have another drink with me while I wait for that call,' Brad suggested, then added with a grin, 'Lucky won't mind if you're late, will she?'

'Madam's nose would definitely be out of joint.'

Erin yawned, but she didn't move. Her weary muscles seemed to have gone on strike. 'All right.' She reached behind her to the fridge for the wine bottle. 'Just a small one. Annie, what about you? Want another drop?'

Annie waved her keys at Erin. 'Sorry, but my boys will be demanding dinner by now.' She winked from the doorway, nodding discreetly at Brad. 'Have a good night.'

Erin cringed. Annie needed talking to. The last thing Erin wanted was for her to start pushing Brad at her every opportunity.

Suddenly the group was down to two. Brad and herself. It felt way too cosy sitting here with him. She studied him from under her lowered eyebrows. Her stomach tightened at the way his sun-kissed hair hung loose, at how his white cotton shirt stretched across that wide expanse of chest.

Whenever she was near Brad she felt like she was in a tumbledryer, free-falling from the top, twisting, turning over and over, never quite touching the bottom.

'Erin? Where have you gone?' Brad watched

her over the top of his beer, his come-to-bed eyes disturbing her further.

Heat rushed up her neck, flowed over her cheeks. He'd caught her staring at him. He had to know exactly what she'd been thinking.

She focussed on her glass. 'Sorry, miles away.'

'You sure know how to make a bloke feel good,' Brad teased.

At least she hoped he was teasing. 'It wasn't a great line, was it?'

'Are you cycling over the weekend?'

'I'll do a ride on Sunday. Probably head out to Picton, around the Queen Charlotte track through the Sounds, then home.'

'That's got to be a hundred ks.' Brad looked impressed, which made her glow inside.

'From home, one hundred and twenty-one.'

'Exactly?'

'Yep. I have a book in which I note down all the distances I cycle and how long it takes me.' She shrugged. 'That's how I keep track of my progress.'

'You take it very seriously.' His chair screeched across the vinyl flooring as he stood up. When he moved around the table her heart rate increased. His proximity caused the air to buzz as if with electricity. As she smelt the fragrance of his skin her mouth watered. Male scent. The best in the world.

Then he pulled open the fridge and she tried not to feel disappointed. Instead she enjoyed the view of his trousers pulled taut across his buttocks as he bent to reach for another beer. When he turned to lock eyes with her she felt her stomach cramp. Shaking her head to break the eye contact, she only succeeded in bumping against his arm. Her muscles froze, her lungs held still. He'd better not be able to read minds. There was a very intense look in his eyes. A look she couldn't fathom. He was so close. That mouth tempting. So, so tempting. And then her libido kicked wide awake.

And she was in trouble. Big trouble.

Brad straightened up, stepped away. He must not touch Erin. Not even in the tiniest way. Despite wanting to haul her into his arms and touch every part of her divine body, he must not. Right now even to inadvertently brush his hand against hers would start a conflagration he doubted he could stop.

The hunger was in Erin's eyes, too. How'd they got to this? So quickly? He groaned. It had been coming from the moment she'd bumped into him in the store. As he moved back around the table he felt as though his skin, his muscles, were tearing at him, trying to stay near Erin. All of him, every last cell in his body, wanted her.

Sinking onto the chair, he pressed his fingers against his eyes, frantically attempting to get himself under control. He should walk out of here right now, go to his office. If he didn't have to wait for the call he'd be on the Harley, putting wind through his brain.

'I'll clean up.' Erin's voice wobbled.

He daren't look up. If he saw that need still in her eyes he would definitely do something he shouldn't. Like kiss those full lips. Like— *Don't go there.*

Did his voice work? 'Why don't you leave that for me to do while I'm waiting?' How was that? Normal voice? Hah, more like the morning after a binge session in the pub. Croaky and dry.

'Okay.' Gratitude coloured the single word. 'I'll go and close all the windows.' How could her voice sound normal?

She wore three-quarter-length pants that moulded to her curvy backside. He sucked air through clenched teeth. How was a man supposed to stay professional around a woman who looked like a goddess?

He didn't know he'd moved. Suddenly he stood in front of her, his hands running through all that silky hair. Her baby blues widened, filled with heat. And then she was in his arms. Their lips came together. Their mouths opened to allow each other in. Their tongues danced around one another.

Brad's hands claimed her face, her skin soft under the rough pads of his fingers. Through his shirt he felt her fingers on his back. She drove him insane with need. His mouth was slick against hers. The taste of her heightened his desire. He needed more of her. Dropping his hands to her waist, he caressed the hot skin underneath her blouse. Soft, fiery, womanly.

When their kiss couldn't get any deeper, any

fiercer, it got deeper, fiercer. She pushed against him, as though trying to get inside his skin. He pressed back into her, the evidence of his desire hard between them.

Her fingers stroked his neck, his throat, racking up the tension in his body. If he didn't make a move soon, he'd implode.

The phone was ear-splitting.

Erin tasted so sweet, her lips swollen with desire. Then she jerked in his arms, twisted away, leaving him aching where her body had touched his. His fingers shook as he picked up the phone.

'Brad, Andrew Pascoe.'

'Hi, Andrew. Thanks for calling me back.' *Your timing is impeccable. I owe you.* 'I want to talk to you about a thirty-year-old woman who's moved here from South Africa. She's pregnant and has haematological problems for which I need some advice on treatment.'

'Because of the pregnancy?'

Brad explained, 'A congenital anaemia that causes an enlarged spleen. She also suffers from gallstones occasionally.'

'Have you got notes from her doctors in South Africa?' Andrew asked.

As Brad talked he watched Erin crossing the parking area to her sporty car. A red one, such a contrast to her sterile house. She was talking on her cellphone, her face neutral. If ever there had been a puzzle he wanted to solve, it was this woman.

Erin snapped the phone off and waved the remote key at her car to pop the locks. The long week was over.

'Erin, got a minute?' Brad called from the back steps as he locked up.

Her antennae had malfunctioned. She should've noticed he'd come outside. She leaned over the car roof, all the better to watch him move across the car park to his motorbike. 'What's up?'

'Are you doing anything tomorrow?'

'I'm helping Annie's husband on his stand at the Marlborough Wine and Food Festival.'

'For the whole day?'

'Until lunchtime. Why?'

'I wondered if you'd like to go to the festival, as

in eat, drink and listen to the bands. I could meet up with you when you're finished on the stand.' His eyes, when he focussed them on her, were fudge coloured, making her all warm inside, and willing to do whatever he asked after all.

'It's the Three Streams stand.'

'That's a yes, then?'

She nodded. 'Definitely.'

'See you then.' He lifted one hand in salute before buckling his helmet on. The Harley roared to life and within seconds Brad was tearing down the drive out onto the street.

Hot damn, she had a date. With Brad Perano. Oh, my goodness. Her feet did a fancy little dance as she watched the bike disappearing amongst the peak-hour traffic. She punched the air, and spun around, hugging herself. A date. With a real man. A really hot man.

Oh, dear. Was that wise? Could she keep up with a man like Brad? Her inexperience would show and he'd wonder why he'd asked her out.

Only one way to lose that inexperience. Her face cracked wide and she laughed. Bring it on.

CHAPTER FIVE

ERIN poured a measure of Chardonnay into a glass and handed it across, taking the customer's coins with her free hand. The festival was really rocking, with people pouring in through the gates as fast as the buses could transport them from town. The annual event attracted people from all over central New Zealand. Three sides of the large grassed area were lined with tents from Marlborough vineyards selling samples of their wines, interspersed with other vendors selling local exotic foods.

Rick's winery had a good reputation and the queue seemed endless. Working alongside Annie and her husband in the tent, Erin screwed the cap off yet another bottle of Sauvignon Blanc as she informed them, 'I'm having a venison burger before much longer.'

'Crayfish for me,' Annie and Rick said in unison.

Then Annie grinned. 'You're keeping someone waiting. A man with a big appetite, if I'm not mistaken.'

Puzzled, Erin turned around to find her antennae had failed her again. 'Brad.' Last night's kiss was still fresh on her lips. 'Do you want a wine? I'm not quite ready to go yet. Waiting for staff.'

'All taken care of.' He raised his hand, a bottle of beer glinting in the hot sun. 'Do you need another pair of hands back there?'

'Yes, please.' Annie didn't need a second offer. She introduced Rick and quickly showed Brad the wines.

Erin tried to pretend Brad was like any other guy as he poured wine for Rick but little flutters had set up in her stomach the moment she'd seen him standing there. He made her nervous in an excited kind of way. Her muscles squeezed as she suppressed a wild smile. She had a date with him, starting very shortly. No wonder she hadn't slept much last night.

'Sorry we're late.' Two men barrelled into the tent. 'The traffic out there is dynamite.'

'That means you two can go and have some fun.' Rick passed two glasses of bubbles to Erin. 'I know you love it.'

Erin accepted the glasses. 'Two?'

'One for Brad.'

'Not for me, thanks.' Brad smiled.

'I'm sure you'll manage both.' Rick winked at Erin.

Brad's eyes were fixed on her in that disconcerting way of his. 'Want to go get that venison burger?'

'Now that you mention it.' Thoughtlessly she ran her tongue over her lips and saw his eyes widen. Stupid woman. He'd think she was seducing him. As if. She didn't do seduction. That would be way too dangerous with a man like Brad. A man who oozed sexual assurance without effort.

About to say something, anything, to break the connection with that gaze, she hesitated. Why not seduce him? She knew how much she wanted him; how her body behaved every time he came near.

He obviously felt that same pull. He'd reacted fast enough last night when they'd been kissing.

Brad nudged her. 'You're daydreaming again.'

Heat coloured her cheeks. What had she thinking? Brad could wreck her carefully put-together life. Safer to stay here serving the endless stream of people wanting to sample Rick's wines.

But that would be taking the coward's way out and one thing she knew about herself was that she wasn't one of those. Being surrounded by the crowd there'd be no kisses today, nothing to snap her wire-thin control. 'Shall we get our burgers and sit where we can listen to the bands?'

'Fine by me.'

'So how is it that with all these amazing wines available you're drinking beer?' she asked as they wandered through the crowd.

'I'm a beer kind of bloke.'

Definitely. Hard to picture a delicate glass in his big, strong hand. Then again, that hand had also felt incredibly gentle and soft on her skin last night. She gulped a mouthful of the sparkling wine and the bubbles rushed up her nose, making her sneeze.

'Beer doesn't do that.' Brad grinned at her.

She laughed, suddenly feeling carefree and happy. Whatever happened, she intended enjoying the day with Brad. 'I'm starving.'

'Me, too.' His voice faded away as he studied a group of people close by.

'Something wrong?' she asked, glancing across at the men, who were staring at Brad, sneers on their faces.

'Nothing at all.' His hand tugged her around in another direction. 'We were on our way to get burgers.'

They had barely moved away when a commotion broke out behind them. Erin spun around. 'Something's definitely not right.'

She headed towards the same men, who were now standing in a circle around one of their own. Through a gap she saw a man gripping his throat, his eyes bulging. And his pals weren't doing a thing to help him. Didn't they understand the guy might be in a serious situation?

Grabbing Brad, she pulled him with her, crying out, 'That man's choking.' About to shove her glasses into the nearest person's hands and go to the stricken man, she felt Brad push past her.

'I'm onto it.' But as he neared the group two men stepped up, preventing Brad getting through.

'If it isn't Perano.' One of them smirked.

'Let me through.' Brad ground the words out.

'Think you're better than us now?' a man in a scarlet T-shirt sneered.

'Joey's choking.' Brad spoke calmly, but Erin could see his hands balling at his sides. 'I need to help him.'

'I need to help him,' mimicked Scarlet Shirt. 'Sure you don't want to run away?'

'I'm a doctor, damn it.' Brad's tone remained steady, but exasperation was creeping in. And real anger. 'He'll be dead in a few minutes if I don't get to him. You want that on your conscience?' And he began to push through.

The men looked at each other, then at their mate now kneeling on the ground, clutching at his throat, his eyes imploring Brad to help him.

A woman next to the men screamed at Scarlet Shirt, 'Get out of the way, you idiot. Joey's bad. He needs help fast. Let Brad alone.'

Reaching the distraught man Erin now recognised as Joey Bryant, Katie's dad, Brad leaned down and slapped him hard on the back with the palm of his hand. Nothing happened. A second blow, and then a third. This time Joey's mouth widened and he disgorged the obstruction from his windpipe.

Relief poured through Erin. What would've happened if Brad hadn't been here? If those idiots had prevented him getting to the guy? They'd only held him up for a few seconds but those seconds could've made a difference.

Squatting, Brad checked Joey's pulse and breathing. 'Take it easy, mate. Try not to gasp air too much. Take slow and steady breaths.' Hell, he couldn't get over those goddamned fools. They could've cost their mate his life. Why? Because they still held a grudge against him.

'Thanks, man,' Joey gasped, despite Brad saying not to.

'That was a hell of a thump I gave you.'

'You're telling me?' Joey's relieved grin was lopsided. 'I didn't recognise you at first, but I'm mighty glad you happened along.'

'So am I. Guess that makes us even now.' Brad returned the grin, recalling how Joey had saved him from a thrashing when he'd once picked a fight with someone much bigger and stronger. Two teens against one belligerent man had only just managed to hold their ground and get away relatively unscathed.

'Still get into fights?' Joey asked.

'Put all that behind me way back when David saved my backside.' Troubled, he met Joey's steady gaze cautiously. 'If I had a chance to re-write that night when you came looking for help from me, I'd do it differently.'

'I hated you at the time. We were young and gung-ho, but since starting up the log-hauling business I've learned everyone has to do what's necessary to survive.' Joey hesitated. 'David Taylor was your ticket out of here.'

'Yeah, but I should've been back before now.' Relieved he and Joey had sorted the past out so easily, Brad stood up, looked at the group sur-rounding him. He nodded at those he recognised from way back. None of them met his gaze at first.

Then one man, Den, took a step closer to him.

'Hey, Brad, we were only giving you a hard time, didn't realise how bad Joey was. Guess we're still a pack of useless idiots, eh?' He extended a hand to Brad.

To take it or not? The temptation to walk away was huge, but if he did that he'd be no better than these guys. He closed his fingers around Den's. 'It's been a long time.'

Some of these men were hardly any better off than they'd been twenty years ago. They hadn't had the benefit of a David in their lives to help ground them and turn them around. And things might've gone differently if he'd stood by them instead of putting his own needs first. Then again, nothing might've changed. Some people were doomed to stay downtrodden.

'Too long,' Joey said.

On the other hand, Joey was the one who'd done really well for himself in the logging industry and, if the stories were true, was now very wealthy. And yet he was still one of the guys.

Unlike himself, Brad scowled. He'd let Penelope dictate where they lived, who they'd socialised with, because it had been easier than fighting her on every front. To be fair, at first he'd loved her so much he'd have done anything for her. But later on it had been too late to repair the broken relationships here in Blenheim.

'Want to join us for a drink?' Den asked, as though expecting to be turned down.

'Yeah, I would.' But he was with Erin today and he wasn't about to wreck that burgeoning friendship as well. Where was she? He glanced around, saw her standing a little way back, watching him in that enigmatic way of hers. 'Can we take a rain-check? I'm kind of busy right now.'

Four pairs of male eyes turned to where Brad's gaze fell. 'No problem, man. We'll give you a call at that fancy medical centre.'

Brad spun back, his hands tightening before he saw the friendly laughter in their eyes, on their faces, and he relaxed. 'You do that,' he said, before strolling back to Erin. 'Let's go get those burgers before you faint from hunger.'

Her fingers stole around his elbow. 'You were great with Joey.'

'Once a doctor, always a doctor. Or a nurse.' He gave her hand a squeeze.

'You know those people from when you were a kid?'

'Yeah, we went to school together, and we hung out in the weekends, partied on Saturday nights. Den was in the same welfare home as I was for a while, too.'

'They seem to resent your success.'

Brad thought about that. 'No, I don't think they do really. I let them down badly when we were stupid teenagers getting ourselves into trouble with the law.'

'I find it hard to imagine you doing anything even slightly illegal.'

'Don't paint a rosy picture of me.' He'd never live up to it. 'I also think those guys probably remember my ex telling them how she'd bettered herself by marrying a trainee doctor and how she couldn't wait to see the back of them. She came from the same part of town as the rest of us and I was her ticket out.'

Erin glanced up at him. 'That's not nice.'

'It's understandable. She didn't think she had any other opportunities.' But that still didn't excuse what she'd done to him later, and he couldn't forgive her for that. Losing Samuel had to have been the hardest thing ever to happen to him. But enough. He was with a beautiful woman, and she felt right for him at this particular moment. 'Let's go enjoy ourselves.'

Brad was surprised how much fun they did have, sitting in the shade of a tree, eating and drinking as the bands entertained the ever-increasing crowds. He couldn't remember the last time he'd done something so ordinary and relaxing. He'd have to do more of it.

Erin sprawled her long legs out and leaned back on her elbows. 'Why were you in foster-care? If you don't mind talking about it, that is.'

He hadn't seen this coming. But why not tell her? It wasn't a secret. 'My parents were killed when I was five.' He picked at the label on his beer bottle. 'It happened late at night at the train crossing in town. Apparently it was as dark as pitch and Dad can't have seen the train coming. Of course there weren't any barriers in those days. I was the only survivor.'

'You were in the car, too?' Horror made her shiver.

Brad picked up her hand, rubbed the palm with his thumb. 'I still struggle to drive across railway lines anywhere. They're unavoidable in Blenheim, though.'

'I can imagine.' Her fingers curled around his hand, pressing gently. 'Didn't you have any relatives to go to?'

'Two elderly aunts in England who weren't interested in a young boy on the other side of the world.'

'How could they not want you?' Her face showed indignation on his behalf.

'I guess when you're in your seventies the whole concept of raising a child is daunting, if not impossible.'

'They could've tried. Surely to be with family, no matter how elderly, is better than going into the state system?'

'I'll never know.' But he'd often wondered the very same thing. 'I went to England a few years ago and met Gertrude. The other aunt had died years earlier. After that meeting I decided I'd probably done better remaining in Blenheim.

Gertrude was a humourless woman with very little compassion.'

'Were your parents English?'

'My dad was. He came out from England when he'd qualified as a doctor to work in the hospital here. That's where he met my mother, who was a doctor there already.'

Erin stared at him. 'To lose your parents when you're so young is incomprehensible. I know my parents haven't been all that parents are supposed to be, constantly putting the army before me, but at least I had them.'

'Eventually I had David and Mary. Without their intervention in my life I might have become an expert at breaking and entering.' He smiled at her. 'Enough of this. We're supposed to be enjoying ourselves. Want to try some crayfish?' he asked.

'Okay, sounds good to me.' The eyes that locked with his were like blue lasers, twisting his gut into knots, tying up his tongue, turning him back into a horny teenager. He shook his head to break her spell.

He leaned closer. 'Want another glass of bubbles?' The scent of her perfume tantalised him, adding to the heady mix of what made up Erin.

'I would but then I might end up a bit drunk and that's not a good look. Anyway there's still a smidge in the bottom of my glass.' She smiled that warm smile that always moved him. She looked more at ease than he'd ever seen her. Because she was having a good time? He could think of ways to have an even better time.

Scrambling to his feet, he told her, 'I'll get the cray. You can continue lazing around.' He moved through the crowd rapidly, putting some distance between him and that alluring woman, sucking in air to make his lungs work, flexing his hands to lighten the tension in his muscles. If he didn't gain control of himself he was going to be a hormone-crazed mess by the end of the day.

'This is delicious,' Erin muttered later around a mouthful of juicy crayfish meat.

Her chin was moist with more juice and Brad leaned across to wipe it away with a paper napkin, barely resisting running his thumb over her skin. 'Yeah, it is,' he drawled, watching a blush colour her face.

Snatching up her glass, she gulped the last mouthful. And sneezed as she had earlier in the day. 'Do you rush all the good things in life? Or just the bubbles?' he asked.

Her eyes widened, and she sat up straighter. Her jaw stopped chewing and she swallowed hard. 'Pass.'

Suddenly he wanted to get away from the crowd, far from the noise of the bands and people shouting and laughing loudly as they got drunk from too much wine and sun. He stood up and reached a hand down to Erin, hauled her to her feet, ignoring the surprised expression in her eyes. 'Let's take a ride out to Rarangi Beach.'

Shock rippled through her. He felt it through her hand in his. He saw it in the widening of those beautiful eyes. Any moment now she'd being saying, no, thanks, and he'd have to walk away. He'd be free of this hot, muscle-tensing sensation gripping him. He'd have lost any vague hope that here might be a woman he could enjoy being with for more than an afternoon.

'I haven't got a helmet. Or a jacket.'

His finger lifted her chin, his eyes connected with hers. 'I brought spare gear.'

'Why? Did you plan on asking me to go for a ride?'

'It crossed my mind.' Earlier in the day when he'd been supervising the boys mowing David's lawn it had seemed a great idea. Back then he hadn't been feeling this lust for Erin. Or had he really been anticipating continuing on from that kiss yesterday?

Reaching up, she touched his cheek. 'Of course I'll come with you. But I have to tell you I've never ridden on a motorbike before.'

Relief poured through him, his shoulders relaxing. She was coming riding—with him. 'It's easy. You just have to hold on tight and roll with me and the bike.'

'Hold on?' It was slowly dawning on her that she'd be wrapping her arms around him, tucking her face against his back. She swallowed nervously.

'It's easy, I promise.' Not to mention exciting.

Erin smiled to herself as she walked beside Brad to the car park and the Harley. She could see other women giving him the once-over, rearranging their bodies into seductive poses. Brad had that effect on her too.

Why had she recklessly agreed to ride with him?

Thump. Thumpity-thump. Her heart played the beat. Would it be possible to ride on the back of the Harley without holding onto Brad? Without touching him? Her cheeks heated. Thump. Thumpity-thump.

The bike roared as Brad sped along the roads bordered by vineyards. Row upon row of vines laden with bunches of young grapes flicked past Erin's line of vision. A line impeded by a broad, leather-covered back. A back she tentatively laid her cheek against, savouring the delicious feeling of belonging in Brad's world for a brief interlude.

At the end of the vineyards Brad travelled around the edge of the town until he connected with the main road out towards the beach. He rode hard and fast, but with a confidence that came from knowing his machine and his own capabilities. Erin totally trusted him and relaxed further, snuggled closer, and kept her arms firmly around his waist. Heaven. To be holding Brad like this went way beyond any recent daydreams because this was for real.

As the engine roared beneath her, Erin tightened her grip and prepared to roll through the corners with him. Her face split into a wide grin.

When Brad pulled into a park beside the wild beach Erin sat dazed, only becoming aware she was still holding onto him when he twisted in her arms and knocked on her helmet. 'How did that go for you?'

Her answer must've been written all over her face because he smiled back so tenderly that the butterflies in her belly woke up. Instantly pulling away from his warm torso, she tugged her helmet off. 'I think I'm going to have to get myself a motorbike.'

Brad chuckled. 'Beats pedalling, doesn't it?' His steady gaze darkened as he watched her. There was a hitch in his voice when he asked, 'Feel like a walk?'

A walk should be safe, and give her time to get these crazy roller-coaster emotions under control. Unless that hitch meant he had other ideas. But studying him, she couldn't see anything that made her think so. 'Sure.'

She slid off the big machine and ran her fingers through her flattened hair, puffing it out a bit. Her face tingled from the air-blasting it had received.

An offshore breeze cooled the sun's heat enough to be comfortable. She slung the jacket Brad had lent her over her shoulder. 'I guess we can't leave these here with the bike.'

'Too right. I don't want anyone turning up and thinking it's their lucky day.' Brad still wore his jacket but hooked both helmets over one arm as they began to walk down the sandbank.

With his free hand he reached for hers, his fingers wrapping around her hand, engulfing it, warming her skin to a dangerously high temperature. The heat flowed up her arm, spread throughout her body, tripped her heart into that erratic pattern again, dried her mouth, rippled down through her tummy, down, down to the junction at the top of her lifeless legs. A deep pulse throbbed there, sending waves of desire outward, upward, making her tremble.

Long-forgotten feelings of desire. No man had

reached past her protective shell since Jonathon, and at the moment she felt more excited than she could remember feeling ever before. And very nervous.

She stumbled.

'Careful.' Brad caught her. Wound his arm around her. Hauled her in against his body.

'This is being careful?' she muttered.

'Not really.'

The gentle slurp and slap of the sea inching forward over the hot sand was in direct contrast to the heavy thudding of her heart. The jacket slid from her lifeless fingers to the ground. Her head tilted back, and despite her nervousness, her lips sought Brad's. She needed his kisses. Badly. As his face closed the gap between them her tongue slicked her bottom lip. Her hands gripped together at the back of his neck, holding her upright.

His lips were warm, firm, all man. They tasted of fresh air. They covered her mouth, moved slowly over her lips, sent fresh waves of desire charging down her body.

She shook uncontrollably as Brad's hands moved across her back, pushed up under her shirt. So much for self-control. Right now she didn't have a drop. His palms, hard and rough from outdoors work on David's property, touched her bare skin. And like petrol to a flame her body erupted.

Someone groaned. Loud and long. Her. Oops, she never made sounds like that when making love. *You're not making love. This is a kiss. Nothing more.* So why was she melting into Brad's body? Why was she trying to get even closer to him? Closer than humanly possible? *Because you want him. All of him. Not just a kiss. Not even a whole load of kisses. You want Brad down and naked, and inside you.*

His mouth still devoured hers. His hands made their way between their bodies, on her skin, making her shake with hot need. When he slid under her bra and rubbed his fingers across her nipples she heard another groan. A deep one. A male one. Her eyes flicked open as her nipples tightened, ached.

She tugged her mouth away from his. Indecision wound through her heated brain. Would she be up to the pace? She'd only known one man intimately while Brad oozed experience.

His face was dark with desire, his eyes filled with passion. Passion that resonated through her body. Her own passion; strong, pulsating, demanding to be fed.

'Oh, my.' This was way beyond anything her imagination had come up with. And they were only kissing and touching. But what amazing kisses. What bone-melting touches. There would no stopping now. There couldn't be. She didn't have the willpower to say no. Neither did she want to. She was ready for this. She had to start living again, putting the past behind her, and this was the first step. A great big step. A very exciting, and scary one.

Sucking a deep breath, she grabbed the front of Brad's jeans and popped the button, tugged the zip down over the huge bulge pressing against the denim.

'Erin,' he growled. 'For pity's sake, we can't do this here. We're in the middle of a very public beach.'

'We can't stop.' She glanced over her shoulder. No one was around. But they were in full view of houses. 'Where?'

Against her ear he muttered, 'Think we can make it to those bushes further up the beach?'

His tongue circled her earlobe, divesting her of all thought.

'Erin?' His voice sounded as if it came from way back in his throat.

Tilting her head sideways to avoid that magical tongue, she gulped. If they could shift molten muscle and bone then, yes, they could make it to the bushes. 'Let's go.' She tugged him along.

Urgency drove them. She stumbled over a mound of wet sand and he swooped her up in to his arms without missing a step. When they reached the low bushes he let her down slowly, sliding her body over his until her feet touched the ground. Spreading the jackets over the bracken, Brad pulled her down with him to sprawl across the meagre protection.

'Should've brought a blanket with me.' There was a mischievous twinkle in his desire-laden eyes.

Erin couldn't care less about having anything under them. She just wanted to possess him, to touch his hard muscles, hold his naked body against hers. Reaching for his T-shirt, she shoved it up, tried to tug it over his head. He helped her, and they got hopelessly tangled in arms and T-shirt.

Brad tipped her sideways and pulled the offending shirt off. His fingers fumbled with the buttons on her blouse as she placed her lips on his chest and began kissing a trail from one nipple to the other, then down over his abdomen.

'Help me here, Erin,' he growled in that deep, sexy tone she loved.

'Can't. Too busy.' Her tongue circled his belly button.

Hands on her head, lifting her away. 'Damn it, woman. I can't guarantee I'll be able to wait for you if you don't stop. I need your clothes off.'

'Great idea.' Who *was* this woman talking? Someone she'd never met before. But Brad brought things out in her that she didn't recognise. It was as though her body had never been touched before. Twisting her head, she took his thumb into her mouth.

His groan was pure passion. Then he was back on his feet, hurriedly pushing his jeans and boxers down those tanned, muscular thighs, revealing all his glory.

He was huge. And ready. Very ready. Her mouth dried, her throat closed. *Wow. I'm not up to this. Brad's going to find me lacking.* Glancing up, she saw his need for her as strong as hers for him, and her hesitancy vanished in an instant. As though without any thought her hand rose, reached for his hot, pulsing sex.

Brad gasped. 'No. Wait.' He tugged her hand away before pulling at her blouse, trying to get it over her head.

Vaguely Erin was aware of a tearing sound as her shirt caught under her chin. She shrugged out of it. Reached for him again.

'Your shorts.' No difficulties there. Brad had them off her before she knew what he intended.

'At last.' She lay back on the jackets and reached for him again.

'You're one impatient lady.' Brad slid his hand between her legs and found her most sensitive spot. 'Very impatient, but I love that.'

Her back arched as he rubbed her. She came almost instantly, crying out as she drowned in heat and ripples of desire. And still he kept touching her, bringing her back for a second wave of desire. Sliding under him, she lifted her hips to accommodate him. Joined together at last, she gave in to their passion.

CHAPTER SIX

UPSTAIRS in her townhouse Erin pushed the bedroom window wide open. Behind the trees on David's property she heard the eager young voices of the two boys on lawnmowing duty, Cain and Tony, chattering to Brad. They'd been waiting on David's front doorstep when Brad had stopped to drop her off at the bottom of the driveway.

Disappointment had enveloped her when she'd realised Brad wouldn't be coming in here with her but was going to talk to the boys.

See? Already you're expecting another round with the man. Making love once doesn't automatically mean he's going to turn up for more. Her heart dipped. Brad was a good lover, a fantastic lover. She'd never known such mind-blowing sex, hadn't even known it was possible.

So naturally she wanted to do it again with Brad. *Brazen hussy. You didn't make any effort to be re-*

strained, throwing yourself at him like a starved woman. She had been starved. She hugged herself. But not any more. So much for being nervous about making love with Brad. She hadn't been able to hold herself back in the end.

They hadn't used any protection, either. She mightn't be able to get pregnant but these days everyone had to be careful about catching something nasty.

One of the boys shouted something and she heard Brad answering, his words indistinguishable but his deep voice reminding her of his hungry lips on her skin. She shivered, then stretched. Her body ached deliciously. A long soak under a hot shower would be the next best thing to making love again.

Glancing at her big bed, Erin pictured Brad sprawled across the sheets. A shower was definitely a distant second. Would they ever make love again? Or was that it? A taste of paradise to torment her for the rest of her life? She'd swear Brad had enjoyed the experience.

Her gaze slid across the bed, stopping on her bedside table and the photo of Jonathon. Jonathon.

Her darling husband who'd loved and cherished her. Guilt should be squeezing her heart, turning her hormones to ice. But it wasn't. She did not feel that she'd transgressed any vows. Jonathon was gone. He'd left her in the most tragic way, and the years since had been long and lonely. She needed male company, needed sex, needed some fun. It didn't mean she'd forget Jonathon. And she most certainly wasn't falling in love with Brad.

Just moving on.

She picked up the photo and stared at the handsome face looking back at her. There was no sign of disappointment in those beautiful grey eyes, no look of condemnation on his face.

'Thank you,' she whispered, then tugged the drawer open and put the photo away, face down.

Hot water pummelled her skin, turning it pink. Too hot for a midsummer's day but as she lathered soap over her body she luxuriated in the heat.

'Any room for me in there?'

Erin jumped. 'Brad. Don't you believe in knocking?' Her heart thumped with excitement.

The glass shower door swung open. 'And have you send me away? I don't think so.'

'As if. If you're coming in then make yourself useful and wash my back.'

'Yes, ma'am.' Discarding his clothes in double quick time he pressed in beside her.

Her breath stuck in her throat. His body was so big, solid, tanned. Beautiful. She laid her hands on the vast expanse of his chest.

'No, you don't, or I'll never wash your back. Turn around.'

'Yes, sir.'

It wasn't easy. Brad took up so much space they had to shuffle around each other, her skin sliding across his as she turned. Instantly she felt that deep, hot need pouring through her again. And when she stood with her back to him his reaction to her was very apparent against her bottom.

A happy sigh tripped across her lips. This would be a shower she'd remember for ever.

Two hours later Erin passed Brad a beer and poured herself an iced coffee before settling at the table. She couldn't hold back her satisfied smile. Sweet exhaustion softened her muscles.

Brad prowled around the open-plan kitchen and

dining area, peering at her photos as he swigged his cold drink. When he studied a photo of her and Jonathon in ski suits for too long she shifted uncomfortably on her chair. Did he regret their lovemaking now? He moved on.

'What's to eat? I'm starving after all that exercise.' Brad poked around in her fridge. 'Any steak? Meat? Man food.'

Slapping his butt, she pushed him aside. 'How about this?' She pulled out a packet of sirloin from the meat drawer. 'Man enough for you?'

Taking her face in his hands, he kissed her mouth. 'Perfect. Let's have a barbecue. I'll bake some spuds while you toss up a salad. What are those? Fresh peas?' He rolled his eyes. 'Yes, please.'

Erin smiled as she emptied half the fridge's contents onto her bench. How long since she'd prepared a meal for a man in her home? *David didn't really count.* So long ago she'd forgotten about much fun it could be. Especially since this was with a man she'd just made love to. Anything else? She surveyed the fridge interior. No other vegetables, but that bottle of Sauvignon Blanc looked enticing.

'Here.' She handed Brad another cold beer and sipped her wine, watching as he expertly turned the steak. 'I think this is the first time the barbecue has been used.'

'I thought it looked too clean. Don't you have friends around for meals?'

'Not really.' Most of her friends were the people she worked with and by the end of the week she didn't need to share her house with them. 'David pops in for dinner once a week, but that's about it.'

'Sounds lonely.'

Shocked, she looked at Brad. 'Not at all. I spend quite a lot of time around at Annie and Rick's. And I belong to a cycling club and we have a ride one evening a week. No way am I lonely.' But today had shown her that there was more to life if she wanted it.

And she definitely did, especially if it involved Brad. One day and she believed they suited each other well. One day shouldn't be long enough to decide that. But she had. Not only had it been exciting, there'd been that intangible something that said she couldn't imagine her life now without Brad featuring in it somehow.

She felt even more sure when she finally dragged her eyes open late the next morning. A heavy arm around her waist held her down on the mattress, a long, muscular leg pinned both her legs so she couldn't stretch out. And gentle breaths tickled the back of her neck.

'Morning,' came a very male grunt.

Erin tried to roll over in his arms but he held her still.

He groaned, 'Don't move, for pity's sake.'

'Why?' Erin held herself still. 'Oh.' Her mouth stretched into a satisfied grin as her backside was nudged by Brad's erection. 'Again?' Was the man insatiable?

'You complaining?'

'Not at all.' She didn't know a man could do this so often in one night. 'Rolling over,' she warned.

But he held her in place. 'Lift your leg,' he commanded.

Then he slipped between her thighs. His hands pulled her against him, his hardness touching her warm opening, teasing, playing, as his hands moved down her stomach, lower into her triangle.

Erin bit her lip as she moved with him, then waves of erotic sensations took over, dominating all her thoughts, filling her with such pleasure she felt she'd become a part of Brad, melting into him, becoming one with him.

Brad flipped onto his back and stretched his arms above his head. Every muscle in his body ached deliciously. What a workout. What a night. The sex had been astonishing. Erin had revelled in everything they'd done, which had surprised him. She'd come across as though she only felt comfortable when she was in control of a situation. But making love turned out to be the exception. There'd been a definite lack of control at times throughout the night.

He grinned, his pride taking a bow. He'd done that to her, given her a good time. He'd had a great time, too. So where did they go from here? It felt good to have a woman enjoy his company. Enjoy his company? How lame was that? She fancied him, that was what. And he fancied her right back.

Run, Bradley Perano. Run before this woman gets any closer. Run while you still can. His stomach tightened. If he'd kept the lid on his desire then he wouldn't have to consider how they moved on from here. A predicament he wasn't ready to face, to make a decision about. But they worked together, damn it. Despite what David had said, he didn't agree about mixing business with pleasure.

Running his hands down over his face, he sighed. He'd put off thinking about all that for now, just gone with the flow and enjoyed the morning with Erin. But he'd have to put the brakes on this fling before it got out of hand and became a full-brown affair.

He rolled onto his side, his muscles protesting. That had been the best night of his life for a damned long time. How could he even be considering not repeating it? Because he had to. Maybe they could finish the weekend together? Another afternoon and night spent making love, having a meal, enjoying each other. Tomorrow was the beginning of a new week and they could move on from this weekend, savouring it but putting it firmly behind them.

From downstairs he heard what sounded like a cupboard door slamming. Then definitely heard a pan on the stove top. Was Erin cooking up a storm? He hoped so. He was famished.

All that exercise throughout the night had worked up an appetite of massive proportions. For food. And maybe another round in the sack afterwards.

Bacon. He smelt it, heard the sizzle. His stomach gave a hollow lurch. Food.

Brad leapt from the bed, dragged on his jeans and staggered downstairs. 'Hey, that smells so good.' He pinched a piece of bacon straight from the pan, blew on it and placed it on his tongue. 'Hmm, that's divine.'

'How many eggs?' Erin flicked his fingers with the tongs when he tried to snatch another piece.

'Two. Are those hash browns?' Then Brad's focus changed. The best thing of the morning wasn't the food. Erin looked gorgeous and sexy in a pair of white shorts and a blue singlet top that matched her eyes to perfection. The cotton fabric outlined the curves of her breasts, reminding him how they'd felt in his hands—warm, heavy, soft. 'Let's forget breakfast. I'll eat you instead.'

She grinned and kissed his chin. 'If I don't have real food soon I'm going to faint from hunger. Somehow I've got to find the energy for a hundred-and-twenty-kilometre bike ride this afternoon.'

'You're what?' Brad stopped pouring the juice she'd placed on the bench into two glasses and stared at her. She was super-fit. He'd felt all those muscles last night. 'Are you out of your mind?' There went his plans for the afternoon.

'Probably. Of course, if you have ideas on how to fill in the day then I'm open to suggestions.' Her lips lifted at the corners as she flipped the bacon and broke eggs into the pan.

'Woman, you're insatiable.' He knew he was, still not having had enough of Erin after an eighteen-hour sex-fest.

Her grin widened till he thought her face would split. 'Plates are in the bottom cupboard.'

'Yes, ma'am.' Bossy britches. He finished filling the glasses, found the plates, the cutlery, then the condiments, and took everything out to the patio table.

Erin followed with the food. 'There you go, enjoy.'

Her plate was nearly as full as his. Where did she put it all? Her stomach was as flat as a board and there wasn't a scrap of fat on her long body. As she reached across for the pepper grinder he was treated to a full view of those beautiful breasts. He swallowed, looked away, forked up some bacon and chewed thoughtfully, wondering why he felt so light, so free.

Happiness. That's what this was. Pure pleasure. A great night making love with a wonderful woman, then sharing a tasty late breakfast. What more could a man want? Damn, next he'd be putting his slippers by the hearth. Rhetorically speaking. A shudder ripped through him. No way. That was picket-fence thinking and he didn't do fences, back yards, or any form of domesticity.

'Have you got any plans for later today?' Erin asked around a piece of toast.

Despite his misgivings, Brad knew exactly how he wanted to spend the rest of the day. Upstairs in Erin's bed. 'You've got your ride to do so why don't we have dinner somewhere in town later and then come back here afterwards?'

Those eyes lit up with anticipation. Erin obviously had no doubts. 'Sounds fine to me.'

So much for keeping her at arm's length. The big question was if he would be able to say no to her after tonight. Or would his body keep craving more of Erin?

Erin threw the duvet off the bed. Punched her pillow. Downed half a glass of water. Sighed. Stared through the darkness at nothing. Checked the bedside clock. Only eleven-thirty.

Where had Brad gone? He hadn't returned any of her phone calls. Hadn't turned up to take her out to dinner as planned. *Hadn't phoned her.* Hadn't done a darned thing.

Returning home from her ride, she'd had a long, hot soak in the shower before dressing carefully in a spaghetti-strap dress that fell in soft folds to just above her knees. The sea-green shade suited her to perfection. It hadn't mattered that her backless, high-heeled shoes added to her height because she'd always be shorter than Brad. It seemed nice not to have to think about towering over a man when she dressed for a night out.

A night out. Like she was supposed to have had tonight with Brad. Where was he? Why hadn't he had the courtesy to call her if something had come up?

An emergency with a patient? Unlikely. Their medical centre shared weekend rosters with three other centres in town. This was definitely not their weekend on duty.

Lucky leapt up onto the bed, stalked across her legs and settled against her tummy. Rubbing the cat's back, Erin was rewarded with a purr. 'At least *you* appreciate me.'

Purr, purr.

She tugged the sheet around her neck and rolled onto her side. Crippling tiredness sapped her muscles, but it didn't help her sleep. Squeezing her eyes shut and forcing her mind to stop thinking about Brad, she breathed in slowly, filling her lungs to capacity. Breathed out. Any minute now she'd fall into a deep sleep. And then she'd wake up refreshed and ready for another day working with Brad.

Her eyes popped open. She flipped onto her back. Brad. *Get out of my head. Leave me in peace.* But he wouldn't go away. Instead she ached to hold him against her, ached to touch his skin, to kiss his mouth, to feel his maleness pressing against her, into her.

Hadn't he enjoyed their night together? Had that look of amazement lightening the brown of his eyes been in her imagination? She'd had a moment of panic wondering if she would be exciting enough for a worldly man like Brad, but that had been dispelled right from the very first kiss on the beach. If anything, she'd behaved too wantonly.

A motorbike roared through the night. A Harley. She recognised the throaty roar that matched Brad's personality. Her breathing quickened when it slowed outside her place. He was calling in to see her. To explain? Or to apologise? She shrugged. He was here; she'd forgive him anything.

Her ears strained for his footsteps.

The bike revved and sped up the drive to David's house. So Brad would park it in the garage before walking down here. He'd be conscious of leaving it outside overnight in case someone decided they wanted to borrow it.

She waited, only breathing when her lungs threatened to burst. She waited until Brad could've walked to China and back.

Brad sat in the lounge of David's house, his legs stretched out in front of him. Midnight had come and gone and still he didn't feel like going to bed. What was the point? He wouldn't sleep.

How could he have been so selfish? How hard would it have been to pop home to see how David was during the day? To have told David where to find him if he needed anything?

Yeah, that would've helped a lot. The man hadn't been able to move, not even enough to crawl out of the bathroom to phone the emergency services. David had fallen badly, breaking a leg and five ribs. He'd been lying on the floor in agony since eight the night before, waiting for Brad to come home.

And what had *he* been doing? Having a wonderful time in the arms of a woman. Totally oblivious to his responsibilities with David. Not only had he taken too long to return to New Zealand, he was still managing to let the man down.

Acid boiled in his stomach, souring his mouth. The shock of finding David shivering and frightened in the bathroom would never go away. He wouldn't be forgiving himself this one. Maybe he had to start considering what David hadn't yet asked of him—moving to Blenheim permanently and taking over his practice. He knew that was what David wanted more than anything, he just didn't know if he was ready to do it.

Brad picked up the phone from the floor, pressed in the numbers for the hospital and got put through to the surgical ward. 'How's David doing?' he asked the male nurse who answered.

'Dr Perano? All David's vitals are good but we're keeping him heavily sedated. He's going to be in some pain when he wakes up.' David had had orthopaedic surgery to pin his femur.

As if he didn't have enough to deal with, having the blasted Parkinson's. Brad tossed the phone down on the couch and banged a fist into the palm of his other hand. Damn it.

Leaping to his feet, he paced the large lounge, up and down, up and down. He owed David big time. Without David hauling him out of trouble and standing up for him as a guarantor, Brad would've eventually landed in really serious trouble. No doubt about it. He'd had such a huge chip on his shoulder back then that he'd take on anyone just to prove he could cope with his pathetic life. He'd felt that since his parents had died and left him to find his own way in life he'd had to show the world he was doing fine.

Foster-care had been horrible; nothing like the family life he'd known until that dreadful day when the most important people in his life had been killed. He'd been told by well-meaning locals to stand tall, be strong. He'd done that all right. But no one had liked the result. Too tall, too strong for most people. He'd gone from foster-home to foster-home.

Until the night he'd stolen David's car. David had stitched up a deep cut on Brad's chin received when the car had crashed. The stitches had been easy to handle. The talking to afterwards not. But the genuine warmth in David's eyes that night, the real concern for a teenager he'd never met before, had broken through Brad's armour like nothing else had.

David had saved him. Turned him around. He'd gone to school to learn, not to disrupt. Somewhere along the way he had vowed to follow in his parent's footsteps and become a doctor. Of course no one had believed he could do it.

Except David and Mary.

And how had he repaid their kindness, their many kindnesses? By dragging his feet in Adelaide when David desperately needed him. Even today he'd lost his mind to a woman and forgotten to make sure David was safe.

Well, one thing for sure. That wouldn't be happening again. His foray into dating had come to a grinding halt. He'd been looking for a reason to slow the pace, halt the fling, but he'd give anything for David's accident not to be the reason he told Erin he was sticking strictly to seeing her at work from now on.

The phone buzzed, causing Brad to almost jump out of his skin. David? Had something gone wrong? Snatching up the phone, he demanded, 'What's happened?'

'Hey, daddy Braddy, you didn't phone me.'

'Sammy.' Brad's heart leapt into his throat, cutting off the air.

'Where were you? I waited for hours for you to call me.'

'Sorry, son.' Was there no end to the people he'd let down today? 'I had to take David to hospital. He broke his leg.' Brad pushed a hand through his hair. 'What have you been up to? How's your week been?'

'We won our football yesterday. Braddy, it's so cool. I get to wear this shirt with big shoulders and tight pants that keep sliding down my butt.' The boy was bubbling with excitement. Obviously he was coping with their separation.

American football was Sam's latest craze. 'Got a photo to email me? I've got to see you in your gear.' And hopefully begin to accept that his kid was turning into a straight-up American.

What he really needed to accept was that Sammy wasn't really his kid. Follow Samuel's example, get a life.

CHAPTER SEVEN

'So how did the hot date go?

'Annie, what are you doing at work on a Monday?' Slowly Erin lifted her head from reading the patient file on her desk, trying to avoid waking up the headache she'd finally quietened with a dose of Panadol.

'Brad phoned and told me about David, asked me to cover for today.'

'David? What's happened?'

Brad appeared in the doorway to her office. 'Meeting in the staffroom for everyone. Now.'

'What's this about David? Is he all right?' Had the Parkinson's suddenly got a whole lot worse?

'I'll tell everyone at the meeting.'

'Brad, David is my friend and neighbour, too. Why didn't you call me?' *It shouldn't have been that difficult. We were on very good terms when you left me to go home while I went cycling.* 'I might've been able to do something for him. For you.' Hurt crept under her ribs. Why hadn't he turned to her? 'You phoned Annie.'

'I need her to cover some of my hours today.'

So Annie was a doctor, she merely a nurse. But she was his friend, *and* his lover. However temporarily. 'I see.'

'David's my responsibility,' Brad told her in no uncertain terms.

Erin opened her mouth then saw the bleakness in his eyes and shut it again. Blast his stubborn pride. David was everyone's concern, not just his. 'You're not on your own,' she muttered.

Brad turned on his heel and strode away.

Annie said, 'David's in hospital with a broken leg. You can hear the rest at the meeting.' She touched Erin on the shoulder. 'So was it a hot date?'

Saturday afternoon seemed a lifetime ago. She dragged out the words. 'Very hot.' And now the spark between her and Brad appeared to have gone cold. Icy cold.

'David slipped in the shower and broke his femur and ribs. He had surgery late yesterday afternoon but of course with his other condition he's taken a bigger hit than most. This morning he was awake and talking, so that's a start.' Brad's voice was clipped, flat, as he reported to all the staff. His gaze was firmly on a spot on the wall somewhere above Erin's head. 'Annie has agreed to cover any hours that I'm up at the hospital, and Ngaire from Redwood Centre is available if needed. As I've already taken over most of David's patients it should be business as usual. Try not to spend too much time talking about this with patients.'

'You haven't got a hope,' Marilyn said. 'Everyone loves David and will want to know how he's getting on.'

Annie added, 'It's not as if people won't have heard. You're forgetting what small towns are like.'

'When did David fall?' Erin asked Brad. There was something he wasn't saying.

His expression hardened, as though keeping his emotions at bay. He headed for the door. 'Saturday night.'

Erin gasped. When Brad had been at her house,

enjoying himself, David had been lying there all that time, in pain, helpless.

Brad was blaming himself. It was written all over his face now that she knew what to look for. 'Brad…' Erin followed him into his office. 'You weren't to know.'

Brad spun around. 'I would've if I'd been there instead of—' He raised his hands in the air, let them drop to his sides.

'Instead of being with me,' she whispered. The affair was over before it had got off the ground. In a stronger voice she said, 'You can't lock yourself up with David 24/7.'

'Can't I?' His eyes glinted at her. 'If I'd been at home I'd have discovered him lying there fifteen hours earlier. Can you imagine enduring pain for that long?'

No, she couldn't, but she pointed out, 'David still wouldn't want you to be stuck in the house with him all the time.' Darn, she'd be begging next.

'Erin, I'm sorry our weekend ended like this but it's best that we know where we stand. I came home for David and I should've been concentrating on that, not having fun.'

That shouldn't hurt, but it did. She'd been a bit of fun, nothing else. No surprises there, but to hear it from him rubbed in the fact that she shouldn't have had any expectations from their extended hot date. 'So you'll shut yourself off from everyone except when you're at work? Who's going to keep an eye on David then, by the way?'

'I'll look into a monitor that he can wear all the time so that if anything happens again he can reach me immediately.'

'What happens when you return to Adelaide?' Or had this made him change his mind about that?

Brad dropped into his chair and logged onto his computer, ignoring her.

She sighed exasperatedly. 'There's a medical supplies company we deal with that have monitors. I'll leave their details on your desk later.'

'Thank you.' He didn't look up from his screen. 'Haven't you got patients waiting?'

Dismissed. Her heart squeezed. She'd been

a fool to think because they'd made love and shared meals that there was something going on between them. She'd been a bigger fool to hope that there might be a future for them.

Brad cursed under his breath as he listened for Erin to close the door behind her. He'd hurt her—badly. Those blue eyes had lost their shine. Her mouth didn't curve upwards into a sweet smile this morning when after their time together she should've been beaming. If only there'd been another way to deal with the situation, one where Erin felt good about everything and he could still do the right thing by David.

He should've called her yesterday, cancelled their dinner date, but he'd been too tied up with David.

That's just an excuse. You could've phoned from the hospital while David was in Theatre.

He'd known yesterday morning that it wouldn't be wise to carry on having a full-blown affair with Erin but he'd wanted just another day, another night before calling it off. Now he had the perfect reason. David.

'Yeah, right.' The mouse in his hand scrubbed over the desk top, his fingers white at the knuckles. The perfect reason didn't equate to feeling happy. But what else could he do? He'd come home for David. If only he'd remembered that before making love with Erin.

He could hear Penelope shrieking at him when he'd found out about her affair. 'It's your fault. If you had more time for me instead of always being at work then I wouldn't have had to look elsewhere for some male company.'

And then again when she'd told him she was leaving him, going to live in the States with the same man she'd had the original affair with years earlier. 'Your fault. You're too busy playing with Samuel or going to work that you don't even know you've got a wife. Well, news for you. I'm taking Samuel with me, taking him to his real father. So now you'll have all the time in the world to concentrate on your job.'

The job that she'd loved telling everyone he held. The job that brought in all the lovely money she so enjoyed, that gave her the lifestyle she'd craved since they'd been youngsters in foster-care. The job that didn't compare to that of a heart surgeon in California.

Brad pushed his chair back on its wheels, stared sightlessly at his feet. That woman had ripped his heart out, left him incapable of loving anyone again.

Outside his office Erin called a patient through to her room. 'How's Molly this morning?' he overheard her ask as she passed the door, her voice a monotone.

Brad dragged his hands over his face, and muttered, 'You mightn't know it, Erin, but I've just saved you a whole truckload of anguish. I'm only capable of looking out for one person or doing one project at a time.'

But his heart felt extraordinarily heavy at the thought of not sharing some private time with Erin. Some fun time, some loving time. For a brief few hours over the weekend it had seemed they belonged together. She was like a drug to him. Filling his veins with her heat, making his skin so sensitive he might have to spend the rest of his life on anti-inflammatories. Teasing him, laughing with him over the silliest of things. He'd begun to feel whole again, as if he might possibly be able to have a relationship again. Squashing that feeling hadn't been easy.

At the moment he had to focus on David's needs. Erin had raised a valid point, one that he didn't want to consider but had to. Who would be on hand for David when he returned to Adelaide? Only last Friday David had hinted that he'd be more than happy to hand over the practice to Brad on a permanent basis.

Brad tapped the desktop with his fingers. This visit was meant to be for only a few months. But now Brad began to think he might be here for a lot longer than he'd first expected. To walk away and leave David again would not be easy.

Probably impossible.

No doubt Erin would be happy to do as much as possible for David if he left, but he didn't have the right to ask that of her. Neither did he really want to. Now that he'd spent some time with David and they'd re-established their old, comfortable relationship, he didn't want to risk wrecking that again. Could he move home long term?

* * *

Brad ushered a very pregnant woman into Erin's room a week later. 'Can you take some bloods from Karen, please? CBC, iron and antibodies today.'

'Sure.' Erin jumped up and cleared the chair for Karen to lower herself onto. 'You've only got three weeks to go, haven't you?'

Karen nodded and wiped a hand across her moist forehead. 'The time can't come soon enough. In this heat I want the little guy out. It's thirty-three degrees Celsius out there.'

'You're having a boy?' Erin thought how she would've loved to have a son. Or a daughter. She'd just wanted a baby. *Still wanted a baby.* Gulp. Not a good idea. Not when she'd be a single parent. Not that she couldn't manage, but children needed two parents.

'We weren't going to find out but when I was having the scan I suddenly had to know. I thought what if something goes wrong and I hadn't learned what sex it was before then, had to find out after it had died?' Karen rubbed her big tummy.

From the doorway Brad said firmly, 'You've got a very healthy baby there and you're in very good shape, so there's no reason for anything to go wrong. Stop worrying and enjoy the last weeks of peace and quiet.'

'I'm a nurse. What do you expect?' Karen grinned across at Brad, but suddenly winced. 'Okay, Toby, settle down. You've already had a game of rugby today.' She fidgeted on her seat, trying to get comfortable, placing her hand over her very extended tummy.

'Starting a rugby team?' Brad came closer. 'My boy used to love rugby.'

Erin risked asking, 'What's Samuel keen on now?'

'Football. The American version.' There was a misty look in his eyes. 'But next month it'll probably be baseball. He just can't get enough sport.'

Karen grinned. 'That's what my husband is hoping for.'

Erin watched Karen's hand rubbing one spot on the side of her tummy. 'Does he kick really hard?' What did that feel like?

'Do you want to feel? Here, give me your hand.' Karen placed Erin's hand against her bulge. 'Just wait, he'll make himself known any minute.'

Erin stared at Karen's pregnant tummy, willing the baby to move. This was the one thing she'd never asked of a pregnant woman, afraid she'd fall apart when she felt the tiny life moving inside. But Karen hadn't given her a chance to back away, and now she didn't want to miss this amazing moment. Something bumped up against the palm of her hand. The baby?

'There, did you feel that?' Karen whispered.

'Oh, yes.' It was beautiful, mysterious. 'Do it again, Toby.' It was her turn to whisper. The baby obliged. Erin's heart swelled. 'That's amazing.' She blinked, bit into her bottom lip.

Don't cry. Do not cry. This was exactly why she'd never asked to touch a pregnant mum's tummy when the baby was moving. She'd get all sad and the longing for her own baby would flare up again. She wanted to have a baby growing inside her, wanted to feel those kicks from the mother's perspective. *This is as close as you'll ever get.*

Another bounce under her hand. She snatched her hand away, turned around and nearly bumped into someone. 'Brad? What are you still doing here?' He'd better not have seen her tears. She turned towards the cupboard, tried to surreptitiously swipe her eyes with the back of her hand. 'I'll take those bloods now. Leave the lab request form on my desk, will you?' And go away.

A warm hand touched her shoulder gently. 'Take a break when you're done with Karen. It's almost lunchtime anyway. I'll put the kettle on for you before my next patient.'

Sure thing, give herself plenty of time to think about the things she hated thinking about. Babies. Being infertile. Wanting Brad back in her life outside work, even though he'd only been missing from it for a month.

She gasped. Why did she mix up babies with wanting Brad? She couldn't be harbouring dreams of having Brad's baby? After just one weekend of passion? Why not? Two impossibilities weren't much harder to handle than one. *Concentrate on the task in hand. Leave these thoughts alone or you'll destroy your carefully put-together control over the situation. The infertility was never going to go away. So deal with it. Get on with taking Karen's samples.*

Her bottom lip hurt as the blood came back into it. 'Thanks, but I've got a load of paperwork to do after this.' She didn't look at Brad for fear he'd see into her heart, read her mind and know more about her than he needed to know. Especially now that he'd made it abundantly clear they weren't ever getting together for a repeat of their lovemaking.

Lunchtime, and Brad called David to see how he was.

'Stop fussing, will you? Spend your time looking out for your patients. And before you say it, I'm not one of them.' David grumped, but he had a point.

Since David's accident Brad hadn't been able to stop worrying about him and continually checked up on him to placate the gnawing guilt that refused to dissipate. Ignoring David's outburst, he asked, 'Want me to get you something from the bakery for lunch? I'm about to go get myself something.'

'You deaf or something, boy? I don't need anything. If you have to be buying food then get

Erin something, feed her up. Last night when she called in she looked like she hadn't eaten in days. Buy her one of those fancy doughnuts you're so fond of.'

Erin with the sad eyes, the tears that she'd managed to smear across her cheeks when she thought he wouldn't notice. Her pain had stung him. That moment when baby Toby had kicked under her hand had brought wonder to her eyes, lit up her face with amazement. And then he'd seen the exact moment when she remembered she'd never know what it would be like to have her own baby kicking. It had been like an eclipse, the sparkle dying in her eyes, turning them midnight dark. That had been happening a lot lately, but at least this time he wasn't the culprit. Her shoulders had drooped, her lips had trembled before she'd bitten into the bottom one so hard it surprised him she hadn't broken skin.

He'd wanted to take her into his arms and hold her tight, to rub her back and let her cry against his chest. His arms had even been lifting from his sides and he'd started to move closer to her when reality struck. To comfort her, to hold her, would only give her reason to think he might be changing his mind about spending time with her away from work. So, fighting down the urge, he'd squeezed her shoulder in a brotherly gesture and told her to go to lunch instead.

Lunch. Doughnuts. His stomach sat up in anticipation as he put the phone down. Maybe he could get Erin one. That would look like a friendly colleague gesture, not an *I really care about you* one.

Better yet, he'd buy enough doughnuts for all the staff then there'd be no doubt about his intentions.

'We've got our second case of meningitis.' Brad spoke from behind Erin.

Her fingers tightened around her pen. When she looked around Brad was leaning against her office doorjamb. 'Who is it this time?'

'Campbell McBride. His father called me out during the night, worried about the boy's temperature and stiff neck. I don't like Campbell's chances.'

She hadn't heard the motorbike. 'Unlike Kyla

last week, then. I believe she's well on the way to a full recovery.'

He stared at a spot on the wall above her head. 'Why didn't Campbell's father call earlier? Or take him straight to ED? Children's lives are too precious. Harry McBride told me he thought Campbell probably had flu. He didn't want to be a nuisance to me or the ED but when he went into the boy's room to turn off the television and couldn't rouse him he got worried.'

Erin shivered. 'That's dreadful. Harry must be beside himself with guilt and worry.' How did parents ever console themselves in these circumstances? She knew she wouldn't ever be able to.

'He's distraught.' Brad sounded as though he blamed himself for not knowing sooner.

'You did your best. If the patients don't call us there's not much you can do.'

'I knew Harry McBride years ago.'

'So you're thinking that's why he didn't phone earlier?' Erin shook her head at him. 'If Harry hadn't wanted to talk to you then he'd have called Annie, or even David. He's not the sort of man to put his son's life at risk because of something that happened years ago.'

'I hope you're right.' He didn't sound like he believed she might be.

Then another thought occurred to Erin. 'I hope this isn't the start of an epidemic.' That was the last thing the town needed. 'Have any other medical centres notified the health department of any cases of meningitis?'

'Not as far as I know. When I admitted Campbell the ED nurse said they'd only had the two.' Brad rubbed his eyes with the palm of his hand.

Her heart squeezed for this man who looked exhausted. Of course he had been called out during the night but did he ever lie awake thinking about her? About their lovemaking? Or had he filed that encounter away in some deep recess of his mind under 'mistake'?

Every night for the past month she'd lain awake remembering the feel of his hands on her skin, his lips on her mouth, on her breasts. Time might be passing but the memories were as intense as ever.

Moving around Brad to get a file from the cabinet on the other side of the room, she carefully avoided any contact with him. But her skin still sizzled with those memories. It wasn't easy coming to work day in, day out, pretending nothing had happened between them. But the way Brad acted towards her she almost believed she'd dreamt the whole thing.

'Are you all right? You look shattered. And very pale.' Brad was watching her thoughtfully. Gone were any traces of worry about Campbell.

'I went on a long training ride last night with a group from the cycling club. They were a lot faster than me.'

'I bet you weren't letting them know that.' He nearly smiled, his lips lifting at the corners for an instant.

'I hate to be the weak link.' But a hard ride on the bike had never made her feel so bone weary. Then there was the nausea she'd been getting occasionally throughout the day.

'You never let a challenge go by, do you? Even when you pay for it later.' His eyebrows rose in that cute way she found endearing. 'Are you sure it's just your training that's causing those shadows under your eyes? They've been there for ages.'

'Lunchtime, everyone.' Annie poked her head around the door. 'Lots of yummy food, care of David.'

'David?' Brad looked startled. 'What's he up to now?'

'Ask him yourself. He's in the kitchen, setting out the plates.' Annie grinned. 'But he did mention boredom.'

'He's still on crutches, for pity's sake. He should be at home.' Brad spun around and disappeared down the hall in the direction of the kitchen. 'David, I need to talk to you.'

Erin looked to Annie and they both started laughing. 'Let's go and listen to this. Should make for a lively lunch break.' Annie grinned.

An hour later the phone on Erin's desk rang, the loud noise hurting her already aching head. As she took down the details of an urgent cardiac enzyme result from the lab nausea gripped her, and then she was rocked by a bout of giddiness. Clutching at her desk, she tried to force the feeling away, but it quickly grew stronger.

'Thanks,' she told the technician, and banged the phone down. She swallowed. And swallowed.

Her mouth soured. She ran for the bathroom. And threw up the lovely lunch David had provided.

When she could trust her stomach again she lurched across to the basin to wash her face. The image in the mirror shocked her. Her cheeks were colourless, making her eyes appear enormous. Lifting her hands, she was surprised how much they shook. What was this? Something she'd eaten? Probably more of the same ennui that had been dogging her for weeks. But to vomit? She shrugged and washed her face.

For weeks. Four weeks. The words lit up her mind like a neon light.

Four weeks. What about them? Oh, no. Not possible. Erin slid down the wall until she sat hunched up on the floor, her body trembling while icy goose-bumps rose on her arms. A month since she'd had sex with Brad.

Desperation clawed at her. She had gastro flu. She had to. She actually wanted to have it. The alternative didn't bear thinking about.

The door swung wide, and Annie burst in. 'Erin, are you okay? Marilyn saw you rushing in here and sent me.'

'I'm fine,' she mumbled, still overcome with the frightening idea pounding her skull. She hadn't had a period in well over a month and a half. She was always very regular. No, there had to be another reason for that. Getting pregnant was impossible for her. Anyway, there'd only been one time Brad hadn't used a condom, the very first time. 'I threw up. It must be something I ate.'

'Yeah, Brad said something similar.'

'Brad?' Panic gripped her. What did Brad have to do with anything? A lot if she really was pregnant. But he couldn't come in here, couldn't see her like this.

Annie sank down beside her. 'We were talking in the hall when you rushed in here.'

'Don't let him in here.'

'Relax, he's gone to his office.' Annie was studying her. 'What's going on?'

'Like I said, it's probably some dodgy food.' She tried to smile, failed miserably. 'Or gastric flu?' she suggested hopefully.

'You'd better come into my office and I'll examine you thoroughly. We'll do a test.'

Erin knew exactly what test Annie referred to.

'Now? Can't it wait until I know for sure this isn't some stomach bug?' She wasn't ready to know the truth, even though deep down she already did. But how could it have happened?

'I'm infertile,' she wailed later as she stared at the pregnancy testing kit. Her heart pounded in her ears accentuating her light-headedness. Squeezing her hands into tight fists, her fingernails dug painfully into her palms. But it was real. She was pregnant.

Annie hugged her. 'Not any more.'

Pulling away Erin raised her gaze to her friend. 'What will I do? I'm single. There's my job that I can't give up. My house isn't suitable for a toddler.' There were so many things to think about.

'One thing at a time. We'll sort it, okay?'

'Thanks for saying "we". I feel very alone right now,' she murmured, and promptly burst into tears. 'How did it happen?' she muttered when she could get coherent words out again.

'You want me to give you a biology lesson?' Annie rubbed Erin's back before sitting down opposite her. 'I presume this has something to do with Brad and that weekend of the wine festival when you disappeared on the back of his bike.'

Erin squirmed. 'Yep. You'd think at thirty I'd know how to take care of myself. It's just that Brad...' She paused, hiccupped. 'He's so damned exciting. Any woman would fall for him. Wouldn't they?'

'Hey, you don't have to justify yourself to me. I'm your friend, remember? Anyway, it's about time you led a more normal life.'

'This is hardly normal.' Erin tried to absorb what was happening to her. She was pregnant. Going to have a baby. She bit the tip of her finger. 'I don't get it. Jonathon and I tried for ages to get pregnant. I only had unprotected sex once with Brad, and I'm pregnant?' Her voice rose, drilling her ears, but she couldn't help it. 'It's not possible.'

'You and Jonathon never did find out why you couldn't conceive, did you?'

'No. We were amongst the high percentage of infertile couples that doctors never find a reason for not being able to conceive. That's why we were about to start the in vitro method, see if the little suckers could get together in a test tube even if they wouldn't play ball naturally.'

'Well, whatever the reason, it doesn't matter now. But you've had a huge shock, and need to sort your feelings out before you tell Brad.'

'Tell Brad?' Ice thickened her veins. 'Tell Brad?' she squeaked. 'Oh, no. I don't think so. Not yet, anyway. I have to get used to the idea myself.' Brad would go crazy. He was mixed up enough as it was without adding a baby to his woes. And he'd been adamant about only dealing with one situation at a time. This one would have to wait until he was free. That was years away.

Annie leaned back in her chair. 'Fair enough, but don't leave it too long. It will get harder to do as time goes by.'

Erin stared at her feet. At least she could see them, but in a few months that wouldn't be possible. 'I don't know how I feel about this baby yet,' she whispered. 'I've sort of got used to the idea that I'll never be a mum. Why else would I be godmother to your three boys?' Lifting her head, she checked Annie out. 'It's weird to think there's a baby growing in me. After all this time, and I wasn't even trying. How dumb is that?'

'Don't get angry with me, but I have to ask. You'll keep it?'

Erin blanched. 'Absolutely.' Her hand crept across her stomach, settled protectively where she thought the baby would grow. Warmth settled over her, melting that chill of moments earlier. Only that morning she'd felt Karen's little Toby kicking and felt gutted that she'd never experience the same thing. Now? Now she would do anything to ensure this little baby growing inside her would be safe and loved. 'This is going to be the most welcome baby in the universe. I love it already.'

Then the chill returned. What would Brad say? Think? 'Annie,' Erin desperately implored her friend, 'please don't say anything to Brad. I need to get my head around other things first.' She didn't know all Brad's problems but she believed the best way to approach him was after she'd made plans—knew how she was going to cope, where she'd live, how she'd manage to keep working. 'Once I've sorted myself out, I'll tell him the news.'

'It's not my place to tell him, but don't take too long. Okay?'

'Okay.' How long was too long? A month? Three months? Suddenly she felt very insecure. The tight control she held over her life had begun slipping the day she'd ridden on the Harley to Rarangi. Now it was running away from her.

It would've been so different learning she was pregnant when she'd been in a loving relationship. Whereas while Brad had been a wonderful lover, it wasn't as though they were in love. Or anything even remotely close.

Something like a question mark settled over her heart. Not love for Brad. It couldn't be. With a deep suck of air she shoved aside the sense there was something here she needed to deal with and concentrated on the only important issue. Being pregnant.

With Brad's child.

CHAPTER EIGHT

'HEY, John, you're looking better every day,' Erin greeted the middle-aged man who'd recently been discharged from hospital. When he was well he ran the local cycling club Erin belonged to. 'You'll be racing us all in no time.'

John grimaced. 'Got to get my bike back first. I don't think my wife's going to be too happy about me getting into the saddle again.'

'Can you blame her after that spectacular crash of yours?'

'Thankfully I don't remember a thing about it.' While out training John had been knocked off his bike by a campervan. He'd been bounced down a cliff, receiving a broken clavicle and ribs, a ruptured spleen and deep lacerations on his thigh.

Erin was dressing those cuts now. 'Did the van driver stop?'

'Yes, thank goodness, or who knows when I'd

have been found.' He gave her a smile but Erin could see the pain and frustration behind it. 'What about your training? Are you doing the race next Saturday?' John asked.

'No, I pulled out. Too much on at the moment,' she fibbed. Riding and nausea didn't mix well. Being pregnant meant she didn't want to do anything that might jeopardise the baby. She was hanging onto Little Blob for dear life.

Annie told her the cycling wouldn't hurt the baby, that it would be good to keep up her high level of fitness. But John's accident only underlined how dangerous being on the bike could be. She sometimes took risks when out cycling, couldn't help herself if it meant she'd beat someone to the finish line. Now the thought she might crash worried her sick. What if she injured herself seriously? A handlebar in the stomach would endanger the foetus. Or a broken clavicle might result in surgery and that wouldn't be good for Little Blob.

No, she'd do anything to keep this baby safe. Anything. Despite knowing too much time had elapsed she'd even worried about the two cases of meningitis, wondering if she could've caught the bacterial infection from Kyla when she'd taken her temperature. Sadness engulfed her. Campbell McBride hadn't made it, the rapid onset overwhelming his body and sending him into a coma from which he'd never recovered.

Beside her John pressed down on the cotton wool Erin had put on the puncture site. 'It's a shame you're not racing. You've improved a lot since last year and I think you'd do a good time.'

'I'd need to.' This year she'd intended taking thirty minutes off her previous time. But even without the danger factor, riding in a cycle challenge didn't hold much interest for her at the moment. Other things dominated her mind. Three weeks had passed since she'd learned she was pregnant, and she still hadn't summoned the courage to tell Brad. She kept holding out, hanging onto the information for another day. And another day. Once Brad knew, the baby would no longer be hers alone. Someone else would have a say in its wellbeing, its future. Even its name.

Which he had a right to.

And he'd get his chance. He had to. It was only

fair. Anyway, her child was not going to grow up only knowing one parent. Neither would it come second to anything else, as she had with her parents. Brad would make a great dad. But he remained so distant with her at times, making it even harder to approach him. Sometimes she wondered if he blamed her for David's fall, which she knew was ridiculous.

She showed John out, passing Brad in the hall.

'Morning, Erin.' He gave her one of his searching looks that instantly had her worrying he'd guessed.

'Hello. There's a pile of results on your desk. And Mrs Cropton wants you to call her about her mammogram results.' She carried on down the hall, then recalled a phone call she'd taken the moment she'd arrived that morning. Turning back to Brad, she tensed. He was standing watching her, deep longing written all over his face.

For her? Her heart rate increased. How could that be? He'd been very clear that their relationship had to be totally professional. No more hot nights. Or days. Not even a meal together at her place. So get on with it, act professionally, ignore those sad eyes. 'Alison called to say Joey can't make the meeting tonight.'

'Damn.' Brad looked annoyed.

'What's the meeting?' None of her business but she couldn't help herself. 'Anything I can do to help?'

'We're meeting with a cross-section of townsfolk to establish a sports club for underprivileged kids like Cain and Tony. It's a way to give them guidance without being heavy-handed about it.'

She sighed. He had ignored her offer. 'That's fantastic. Any sports in particular?'

He laughed, his eyes suddenly lightening up with enthusiasm. 'Come on, woman, there is only one sport. Rugby. Maybe league later on.'

'And here I was thinking I could interest some of them in cycling.' Without getting on a bike herself, of course.

'Cycling? No way. Not for these guys.' Still laughing, he headed for his office.

Erin stared after him. She hadn't heard him laugh about anything since he'd told her they were no longer involved with each other outside work. Obviously this sports-club thing was cheering him up. She should feel grateful Brad's attention was elsewhere, making it easy for her to pretend he was too busy for her to lay this new situation on him. But contrarily she wished he'd found that happiness with her. He'd said he had to devote his free time to David and yet he was planning for a club for kids who would demand a lot of his time.

So that had been his way of saying they'd had a nice time but he didn't wish to repeat it. Because, in his book, it hadn't been that great. Her eyes misted. Her stomach ached. She was falling in love with the wrong guy, a man who would never love her back. Life had thrown some curve balls at her. First she hadn't been able to get pregnant with her husband, then when she had conceived it had been with a man who didn't want to share her future.

Would he want to share his child's? He had to.

None of this conjecture helped. When she finally did tell Brad about the baby he was going to be furious with her for holding out on him. Who could blame him? He had every right to know. So why not go and tell him? Right now?

Selfishness. Pure and simple. For so long she'd

wanted a baby; for years she and Jonathon had done all they could to get pregnant. She'd lost Jonathon because of her drive to have a child. And now that it had happened she wanted to keep it to herself for a while, to hold onto the joy before reality kicked in and made life difficult. The moment other people knew, Brad in particular, this wasn't going to be about her and her baby any more.

Which was being totally unfair on her baby's father.

Tonight. She'd tell Brad before he left for his meeting.

The last patient shut the front door behind him and Brad returned to his office. He needed to phone the hospital about an elderly patient he'd admitted earlier in the day. As he reached for the phone he knocked a small leather folder to the floor. Retrieving it, he opened it and gazed at Sammy's beaming face.

His heart twisted. 'I miss you, boyo. So much you wouldn't believe.'

A loud knock interrupted him and he glanced up to see Erin entering. As usual she took his breath away. He'd relived that weekend with her a hundred times and still not got over her. If anything, his feelings for her had grown. He cared about her. That was all. That was all he could feel as he wasn't about to risk giving his heart to her.

Erin asked, 'Have you got a spare minute?' and purposefully closed the door.

'Of course.' This looked serious. His stomach sank. He hoped she wasn't about to tell him she was leaving for a job elsewhere. The medical centre needed her. He needed her. He leaned back in his chair and looked at her, trying hard to appear unconcerned.

But then her gaze fell on the photos he still held. 'Is that your son?'

'Yes.' Brad's gaze returned to Samuel.

'You must miss him terribly.'

'Indescribable.' Pictures opened up in his head, bright images of his boy laughing, chattering on non-stop, crying when he knocked his knee on the corner of the coffee table.

'I can't begin to imagine what it must be like to have a child and never see him.' Her head shook slowly from side to side.

'Yeah, not being there to watch him grow, to teach him how to ride a bike, to him take fishing, just to be there for him, gets unbearable at times.' Brad put the photos down on his desk, shoved his hands behind his head, interlacing his fingers tightly. Why had he told her that? He didn't usually talk about Sammy to anyone, preferring to hold his grief close. Besides, he didn't like people to know how Penelope had cheated on him.

She asked softly, 'Do you talk to him often?'

'Every Sunday night.'

Her eyes widened. 'That explains your trips on the Harley.'

'It's my way of getting away from the things that haunt me.' After every call he had to get out, ride like the devil chased him, stifle the crippling pain in his heart.

'Does it work?' Erin sat down opposite him in the chair patients used.

'Not one iota.' Not a chance after Penelope's deceit. He reached for the photos to put them in his drawer. Time to see what Erin wanted to talk to him about. But he took one last look at Sammy, and smiled. 'Good-looking little guy, isn't he?' He could hear the pride his voice.

Erin leaned closer, reached out for the photos, studied them. 'He's gorgeous.' Raising her head, she grinned at him. 'Nothing like his dad, though.'

Her comment sliced through him. The old, familiar bitterness rose, souring his mouth. 'He's very like his father. His real father.'

She jerked back, shock radiating from her eyes. 'What do you mean? Sammy's not your boy? But you told me you had a son and he now lives with his mother.'

The bones in his fingers clicked under the tension he exerted on them. Damn, he was an idiot. He had no choice now but to finish what he'd started, otherwise there'd always be a question in her eyes every time he saw her.

He snapped out, 'Samuel's not my biological child.' Not that he cared about that small detail, but it was the detail that had caused him so much heartache. The pain tightened, making his stomach ache. 'As far as I'm concerned, he is my boy. I was there when he was born. I raised him until nearly two years ago. I love him more than anyone in the whole wide world.'

He hated the compassion in Erin's eyes, didn't need her sympathy. 'Penelope, Samuel's mother and my ex, had an affair during which Samuel was conceived. At the time she led me to believe he was my child. I only learned the truth when she told me she was leaving me and taking our son with her, back to his real father.'

Erin's sweet mouth fell open. 'Oh, Brad. How did you cope?'

'One minute at a time. When—' He stopped, withdrew the derogatory word he usually used for his ex. 'When Penelope decided to leave me for the cretin she'd had the affair with she had DNA tests done on him and Samuel. Ammunition for taking my boy from me. Legally I didn't have a leg to stand on and, believe me, I tried everything. The courts did give me some access rights, weekly phone calls, an occasional visit.' They'd never be enough, but it wasn't as though he had any choice.

'It must be tough on Samuel. Does he know that this other man is his real father?'

'It has been explained to him but how much he really understands is hard to tell. He's six so maybe he gets it. He calls the jerk "Dad".' Brad's voice cracked. He pinched the top of his nose in an attempt to hold back the threatening tears.

Embarrassed, he turned away. Samuel called him Braddy Daddy now. Slipping further away from him.

'And I thought I'd had problems.' Her chair scrapped on the floor. 'I really should go.'

He watched her slip out the door, heard the gentle snick as it closed. He'd talked far too much, told her way too many things about himself that he didn't usually share, even with David. But something about Erin did that to him. She was easy to talk to.

Hell, he hadn't found out what she'd wanted to talk to him about. He'd stroll down to her town-house after the meeting. His emotions should be back under control by then.

'Have you told Brad yet?' Annie sipped her wine and settled comfortably into the chair on Erin's patio after dinner that night.

'I'm still in one piece, aren't I?' Erin stared into the bottom of her glass of juice. No wine for her any more. Shaking her head, Erin tried to smile, couldn't. 'Sorry, that wasn't fair to Brad but I'm trying to make light of the situation.' As if she could.

After his revelation about Samuel's real father earlier that day she'd been grappling with the whole scenario. After the trick his ex-wife had pulled, Brad would struggle to believe this baby was his. He knew about her infertility, would remember they'd used protection all but one time. What were the odds of her conceiving that once?

Whatever they were, it had happened. And she had to tell him. A chill settled over Erin. Brad wasn't just going to be angry at how long she'd taken to tell him, he was going to hate her.

Annie nibbled on a cracker smeared with pâté. 'This is heaven. Peace and quiet. I do love it when Rick takes the boys to do male bonding things.'

'As in kicking a soccer ball around.'

'You got it. I'm never going to admit I played for my school soccer team when I was thirteen and just discovering boys. If Rick found out he'd have me out there kicking and chasing that ball for ever. I think he wants his own team.'

'That means more babies.'

'That means he can borrow friends' children.' Annie chuckled and sipped more wine. 'Honestly, though, I think Rick would be over the moon if I said we were having another baby. He loves babies.'

'And the little boys they've grown into,' Erin mused. Did she want a boy or a girl? Did she even care as long as it was healthy? 'How soon can I have a scan?'

'I thought you didn't want one.'

'Changed my mind. It would be kind of cool to know what sex Little Blob is.'

'You mean is it going to drive a red sports car or ride a Harley when it grows up?'

A Harley. A picture of a tiny version of Brad swam through her mind. How cute. He'd be a right handful.

Loud knocking intruded on their peace. Erin sat up. 'Who's that?' She leaned over the side of her chair in an attempt to see around the corner.

'Can I come in?' Brad's voice boomed through the house.

Brad? What did he want? Erin leapt off her chair. She didn't want to see him, certainly wasn't ready to tell him now. She looked desperately at Annie for help, but Annie was scrabbling out of her chair.

Erin squealed at her. 'Where do you think you're going? You haven't finished your wine yet.'

'Home. I'm giving you some time alone with Brad.'

'I don't want time alone with him,' she snapped, her heart banging against her ribs. Her breathing was rapid, her hands clammy. But she had to do this.

'You can't put off talking to Brad much longer, you know.'

Why didn't Annie come right out with it, tell Brad herself if she was so darned concerned? Annie could save her the trouble. Because there would be trouble. Brad wouldn't take the news lightly.

'Easy for you to say.'

Annie slipped her shoes on and disappeared

around the corner of the house with a wave. 'Tell him and get it over with.'

'Thanks a bundle,' she muttered angrily under her breath. This was supposed to happen when she was ready, not when her friend decided.

'Tell me what?' Brad filled the doorframe, his big body looking larger than ever. 'What did you come to my office to talk to me about?'

Erin couldn't interpret the glint in his eyes, and didn't like the question any more when he repeated it. 'Tell me what?'

'I'm pregnant.' There. She'd told him. Badly. Baldly. She shivered. If Annie hadn't put her in this predicament, she'd have done a much better job of it. *Yeah, sure.*

'You're what?' Brad's eyes widened, his mouth tightened.

'I'm having a baby.' Her palms hurt where her fingernails dug in. 'Our baby.'

'You said you were infertile.' He took a step onto the patio.

'Apparently not.' Erin took two steps away from his towering frame to put some distance between them. 'Maybe I never was, and my husband had the problem.'

Brad went from stunned to furious. 'You're saying this baby is mine?'

She gasped. 'Who else's would it be?' She was shocked but given his history she'd half expected this. It still hurt.

'You tell me,' he snarled.

'Thanks a million.' Did he really think she'd been sleeping around with other men? Her sex life had been going through a drought, broken only for one day and night. 'You can be a right charmer when you want to be.' Then her defence mechanisms really cranked up and she attacked. 'For the record, I do not sleep with more than one man at a time. In fact, I don't normally have a man in my bed at all.' Seemed she'd made a huge mistake letting this one in.

'Oh, yeah?' His sneer hurt more than anything.

'Yes, and now I remember why. Like some men, you're fine when everything's all fun and games, but the moment the going gets tough you want out. You don't want to take any responsibility.' Like her father, who'd always gone off on some darned army exercise the moment she'd needed him. Erin stabbed a finger in Brad's direction. 'It's your lucky day. I am pregnant. It is yours. But that's as far as it goes. I want nothing more to do with you. You can go now. You're not needed.'

Liar, liar. The word reverberated around her skull. She needed Brad more than she'd ever needed a man. Or anyone for that matter. Her unborn child needed him. Needed a dad.

And she'd just blown any chance of Brad considering that. Really exploded any hope he might come round to see things from her perspective.

'That all part of your scheme?'

'What?' She gaped at his stormy eyes, his white face.

'Quite the act you're putting on.' Another step closer to her and he bent forward so his eyes were inches from hers. 'You're too late, Erin. I've already learned that lesson, remember? I was taken for a fool once. I won't be taken in again. If you're looking for a good lifestyle for you and your child, find another gullible idiot. I'm sure there's some poor fool out there who'd be beguiled by your sexy body. But don't come knocking on my door.'

Brad spun around, knocking a chair sideways in his haste to leave. His back was as straight as a pole, his shoulders wrenched so far back they should've dislocated. His hands were hard fists at his sides as he stormed through her home and slammed the back door hard, making everything shake.

Silence fell over the place. She slowly dropped onto a chair and wrapped her arms around her legs, hauling her knees up against her chest. Her teeth bit deep into her bottom lip as she tried to stop the quaking in her muscles. Her chin banged onto her knees, snapping her teeth together, pinching her lip painfully.

But that pain didn't begin to compare with the pain in her heart. Unbelievable torture twisted her insides, stewed her belly, and created acid that burned deep into her soul. Would it erase her new knowledge? She fervently hoped so. Because she couldn't face the truth. Truth that had only shown its face when Brad had stormed out.

She loved him. Totally. Despite all his faults. Maybe because of them. He was big and strong, intense, kind, careful and caring. She repeated the litany that sounded, felt, different with her new knowledge.

She loved this man who didn't know how to trust. He believed she'd deliberately set out to deceive him. Brad loathed her now. His eyes had been spitting his disgust for her. And yet she loved him.

When had that happened? How had it happened? On Rarangi Beach when he'd made such passionate love to her that she'd thought she'd died and gone to heaven? When he'd thanked her with a big smile because she'd baked chocolate cake for the staff? When he'd nearly cried earlier in the day because of his son and what his ex had done to them?

Her arms tightened around her knees. What did it matter where or when? She loved him. For all the good that would do either of them. Brad wouldn't be coming within miles of her now.

A deep roar penetrated her bleak thoughts. The Harley tore down David's drive. She realised she'd been listening for that sound, knew that the first thing he'd have done after leaving her would be to leap on his beloved bike to go and get some wind in his face. He loved that Harley; it took him to places no human could. It helped him burn up his pain and anger. It took him away from her and what she'd told him.

As long as he was careful out there. She knew he'd ride fast, way too fast.

'Please be safe.' She couldn't bear to lose another man she loved. Tears flowed down her cheeks, dripped onto her arms. 'Please look out for yourself as you won't let anyone else.'

CHAPTER NINE

BRAD rode hard, trying to leave Erin's words behind. But they stayed with him. Slamming into him every time he powered round a bend in the road. Erin was pregnant. A baby was coming.

He was the father.

So Erin said. How could she believe he'd fall for the same trick twice? She must've forgotten she'd told him about her infertility. Somehow that didn't gel. She was not stupid.

Had she told him the truth? She couldn't have. He'd never intended having more children, and if she was carrying his child she'd taken away his right to make that decision.

The Harley rocked as he jerked his head sideways. Pulling in a rough, angry breath, he concentrated on riding, bringing his speed down to the legal limit, though his mind screamed out to let go, push the bike to the extreme. Let the wind whip away the disbelief, the paralysing confusion.

How could this happen? Again? What was so wrong with him that he was attracted to women who loved to destroy him? Relished in pulverising his heart?

Erin hasn't tried to destroy you.

The hell she hadn't. Laying the baby trick at his feet wasn't designed to ruin his carefully put-together peace?

You call that peace? When every night you can't sleep because you miss Sammy so much? When every time you see a child hurting or ill you worry about your boy? Look how you fell apart at the roadside when you came across young Jason's accident.

None of this had anything to do with Erin and her pregnancy. So much for keeping their relationship on a professional footing. This was as far removed from that as it was possible to get. Recently they'd even started to relax around each other again, then this had happened.

A car charged out of a side road, cutting him off. Brad braked sharply, skidding slightly sideways.

His heart hammered in his chest. He concentrated on controlling the bike. Wasn't going to let it end like this. An accident because he'd lost his temper would be stupid. Fortunately the Harley had the power to get him safely out of the situation.

The car sped away and Brad swallowed the impulse to chase after it and give the driver the biggest telling off of his sorry life. Hardly fair when most of his anger was directed at one particular woman.

Or was he angry at himself? For not believing Erin. For being afraid to face the consequences of her news or of having a family again.

He pulled up on the side of the road to catch his breath, and get his emotions under some semblance of control. It was plain dumb to ride when feeling this mixed up.

You always ride when you're upset.

He revved the throttle.

What if he *was* mistaken about Erin and she'd told him the truth? A DNA test would prove it once and for all. *As it had with Sammy.* If this baby was his, did he want to miss out on watching it grow up? A lump formed in his throat. His heart squeezed. A child. His child. How could he not want to be there for it throughout its life? He'd loved being a dad. That completely unequivocal love that he'd given Samuel, and received back.

If the baby was his then he'd hurt Erin big time. Again. Did he really believe she'd lie to him about something so important? Tipping his head back, he shouted at the stars, 'I'm sorry, really damned sorry, but I don't know what to think.'

Erin wasn't Penelope. She wasn't needy, had got on with her life after the loss of her husband, had dealt with the infertility issue. Yeah, right. By becoming pregnant. With him. Apparently.

He gunned the bike, pulled out onto the straight road and raced towards Picton and a pub. A few beers might blot out the pain for a while.

Might also give him a hangover and that would be very irresponsible when he had patients to see in the morning. It also wouldn't solve a thing. Not to mention not being able to ride back home and so not be around in case David needed him during the night. One beer? No. He wouldn't stop at one.

At Picton he turned off and headed up Queen Charlotte Drive, using the tight corners to focus on while trying to put Erin's news aside for a while. It didn't work.

Okay, if he accepted the baby was his, what next? Would she expect him to marry her? Somehow he doubted she'd settle for marriage without love. And if there was one thing he was sure of, it was that he didn't love her.

Truly?

The bike slowed as he struggled with this concept. Hell, no way. He couldn't love her. He hardly knew her.

Ever heard of love at first sight? Remember how you felt when she slammed into you at that corner shop the very first time you set eyes on her?

That was lust.

And he was a blind man.

Pulling off the road, he sat astride the bike looking out over the dark sea below. His mind was in too much turmoil to ride safely. If Erin took the kid away, as his ex had taken Samuel, would he survive the pain? To lose a child once had been agony, but a second time? Unthinkable.

To accept his responsibilities put his heart at risk again. He already had David to look out for. Add in a child and he'd make mistakes. Look what had happened to David when he had spent the weekend with Erin. But did he have a choice? Could he turn his back on his child? Or Erin?

Erin heard Brad's bike long before it turned up the drive to David's house. In the still night it sounded louder than a jumbo jet on take-off.

She slammed the dishwasher closed and spun the dials for a wash cycle. Had he solved anything while haring around the roads in the middle of the night? Had he come to his senses and realised she hadn't been fabricating anything about her pregnancy?

'Seen any pigs flying lately?' Erin asked Lucky.

Peering through the oven window, she checked out her cake. An apricot layer cake in the making. The staff would devour it in a fraction of the time it had taken her to prepare.

Heavy footsteps clumped up her path. Brad. Who else would come here at two in the morning? Harsh rapping on her back door made her heart jump. Did she want to see him? That depended on what he had to say.

He was in for a sight. Dressed in her old, comfortable robe, she looked a frump. Come to think about it, Brad probably wouldn't notice anyway.

The rapping became pounding.

Flicking on more lights, she made her way to the door and opened it. 'You'll wake the whole neighbourhood with that racket.'

'Tough.' He brushed past her and headed for the lounge.

Slowly closing the door, she followed, her heart heavy. Brad's grim face did not give her hope for the next few minutes. For the rest of her life. Because whatever the outcome of their discussions, and there would be many, the baby was here for ever. Whether Brad had any part in its life or not. She really should have that scan so she could stop calling the baby 'it' or Little Blob.

'Where are the photos of your husband?'

Startled, Erin stared at Brad. 'What does that have to do with anything? Or you, for that matter?'

He shoved one hand through his unruly hair, the other on his hip, pushing his leather jacket askew. 'I'm wondering if you'd put them away before or after you found out you were pregnant.'

'There's one in the dining annexe of Jonathon and I on a skiing trip to Queenstown. I put the others away about a week after you and I went to Rarangi.'

'Why?'

'Because it was time. It has nothing to do with the baby. Or me trying to con you into whatever you think it is I'm after.'

He dropped onto the couch so heavily she feared for it. He said quietly, his voice clipped, 'We still have to work together. I don't want any of the staff knowing about this.'

She gasped. 'That's the most important issue?'

And she'd thought he might've come to his senses. Or was he getting the practical stuff out of the way first? Her heart ached for a man who'd put the day-to-day issues before the big, important ones. Before his baby. Brad was in a bad way if he was afraid to face the truth, especially when that truth might be what he really wanted deep down.

'Hardly.'

'I won't be able to hide the fact I'm having a baby, but I have no intention of telling anyone you're the father, if that's what's worrying you.' He should be more concerned about her health, about how the baby was growing. How she'd look after it. If she'd be a good mother.

'Annie knows.'

'Annie's my closest friend, and my GP. She's not going to be telling all and sundry.' Might as well let him know the rest. 'I will tell my parents that they're going to become grandparents. They have a right to know.'

He shot up from the couch. 'Your parents? Do they live in Blenheim? What will they say?' He slammed both hands through his hair.

'Mum and Dad manage an apartment block in Surfers Paradise, where they moved to after retiring from the army. Mum will ask how I'm keeping and if I'm looking after myself properly. They'll probably ask if I'm being wise having a child, and they might even offer to help.' Actually, that was doubtful. 'Did you think I'd keep it a secret from them?' Like, how?

He began pacing across the room. 'I'm still getting my head around the fact that you're having a baby.'

Was that a start? Or was that as far as he was prepared to go with this? 'Do you accept it is your child?'

His eyes bored into her. 'No, I don't, but…' he shrugged. 'In all honesty I don't know what to think. I never intended becoming a parent again.'

She stared back at him, saying nothing. Waiting. She had to be patient. More patient than she'd ever been in her life. Right when her world had been turned upside down, when she wanted to shake Brad until he saw the truth. He'd lose out on so much if he didn't. 'Do you want to believe it?'

His gaze slipped sideways, returned. 'Again, I don't know. If it's mine, I'll provide for you financially. That goes without saying.'

'Does it?'

Brad said nothing and suddenly tired of trying to be reasonable she snapped, 'Until you do make up your mind, we have nothing further to discuss. I'll take care of everything. This is obviously my problem.' She locked angry eyes with his. 'For the record, I want this baby more than anything. I will do anything and everything necessary to keep it safe and happy and well cared for.' But was she up to it? She wouldn't be happy just being an adequate mother, she wanted to be a super-mum.

'Funny, but that's the one thing I'm certain of.' His gaze drilled into her, driving home his words.

'Thank you for that, at least.' The cloud pressing down on her brain thinned a little. Strike one.

Brad plonked back in the chair, dropped his head into his hands. 'But you have to know I won't get involved emotionally. Having Samuel taken away broke my heart.'

'I can understand that.'

'Do you?' He lifted his head to stare at her. His eyes drilled into her. 'How can you possible understand how I feel?'

'I want to share the baby's upbringing with you.' Studying Brad's face, his fear was apparent so she added, 'I would never take your child away from you. I couldn't. A child needs both his parents, and certainly doesn't deserve to have one taken away from him.'

But of course he knew all about that too, having lost his own parents when he was so young.

He looked lost, confused. Her heart expanded, letting him get to her. She loved this bruised man.

She could help him heal, if he'd allow her close. Together they could move forward, create a happy life with their child. Thoughtlessly she reached a hand to his face, smoothed his cheek.

Brad jerked back, breaking the contact. 'Don't.'

She wrapped her arms under her breasts, suddenly desperate for him to go, to leave her to think things through.

'Brad, it's really late and we have to be at work in a few hours.' As if she was going to get any sleep, but she needed her house back to herself. The urge to cry was taking hold and the last thing she wanted was for Brad to see that. Crying was private. Anyway, he'd probably think they were crocodile tears.

'Brad,' she snapped, when he didn't move.

Ping. Ping. Ping. The oven timer sounded loud in the room.

Brad looked around, sniffed the air. 'You're baking a cake? In the middle of the damned night?' He shook his head at her. His voice dropped to a silky, caressing tone. 'Oh, Erin, a cake isn't going fix this problem.'

'No, but it gave me something to do when I

couldn't sleep.' She blinked. And blinked again. Frantically trying to keep the tears at bay. His words, his tone had reached deep inside her, tearing at her already damaged heart. Blindly she headed to the kitchen and removed the cake from the oven. Tears dripped onto the bench.

Without turning to look at him, she pleaded, 'Please go away.' She couldn't take another minute in his company. Having Brad witness her completely falling apart was not an option.

'I'm off. But at the moment the only thing you and I have in common is the medical centre.'

And the great sex that led to this predicament, but she didn't think he'd appreciate her pointing that out.

'Henry, come through.' Brad called his first patient of the day, stifling a yawn at the same time. Sleep had been impossible after Erin's bombshell last night. 'How's the chemo going?'

Henry took his time settling onto the chair then looked up at Brad. 'Awful, thanks very much. But I'm done for a while. Hopefully for ever, but guess that's too much to expect.'

'Hard to say with multiple myeloma. Many people go into remission after the kind of treatment you've just had.' He was shocked by how gaunt and pale Henry had become.

'It's the staying in remission I'm interested in. Haven't got time for a relapse, too much planned.'

As Brad wrapped the blood-pressure cuff around Henry's arm he asked, 'You're not still going on that European trip you mentioned the first day I saw you?'

'Yes, laddie, I am. I promised my wife and I don't break my promises for anything.'

'Good on you. But—'

Henry held up his free arm, his hand out in a stop sign. 'But nothing. I've talked to the oncologist and his advice is to go for it. If I get ill again while we're away then I'll hop on a plane and be home within thirty-odd hours.'

Brad listened to Henry's blood thumping past the cuff, took note of the readings. 'Nothing wrong with your blood pressure. If it weren't for the myeloma I'd say you're the healthiest sixty-five-year-old I know.' Brad glanced at Henry, and added, 'And, yes, I do know a few. I live with one very stubborn one, for starters.'

'How is David? I heard he had a fall. Silly old coot, needs to be more careful.' Henry chuckled.

'He's being as bolshie as ever when it comes to looking after himself. Says he can manage without my help, but if I'd been there when it happened he wouldn't have had to spend the whole night lying on the floor in pain.'

'And you've been beating yourself up about that ever since.'

'It was my fault.' Why couldn't Erin understand that he couldn't look after David properly *and* be there for the baby? It was difficult enough worrying all the time if David had fallen again.

'If Mary was still alive she wouldn't have given up her bowls or her quilting group to stay home with David. And we all know how much time those things took up.' Henry reached across and gripped Brad's arm. 'You can't lock yourself away, laddie. Before you know it you'll be an old codger like me and not have done half the things you want to.'

Like what? 'I came home for David. I don't have

a to-do list other than seeing him through this damned Parkinson's.' Huh? See David through the illness, not just a few months? When had he made that decision?

'You should have some goals,' Henry growled in his best judge's voice. 'When did you last go out for the evening and have some fun? And I'm not talking about that sports club you and Joey are organising for the boys either. Which, by the way, impresses me. I'd like to help out financially.'

Brad's head swirled as he tried to keep up with his own revelation and the judge's statements. 'We could do with some paint for the clubrooms, thanks very much.'

'I'll write you a cheque before I leave.' Henry's eyes twinkled. 'Better than that, I'll call in and spend a few hours with David tonight. I'll leave the cheque at the house then.'

Brad laughed quietly. And he'd thought he'd avoided the question about going out for some fun. Instead he'd been set up by a very astute man. He was meant to go out tonight. Like where? Meet Joey for a beer some place? No, he'd stay here at the centre and catch up on some paperwork. How boring was that? 'Let's get your shirt off so I can listen to your lungs.'

'I'll take that to mean you won't be at home when I call on David?'

Brad ignored him, concentrating on the old man's lungs, which sounded very healthy. 'You can get dressed again. You're in better nick than me.'

But when he sat down at his desk he could feel Henry's eyes boring into him. 'What?' He turned to meet the steady gaze, the kind of look Henry had used when handing out sentences in his court-room.

'I mean it when I say you've got to grab every opportunity. Look at me. Thought I had all the time in the world to travel, to put in the rose garden I've always dreamed of, to catch the big trout.' The gleam in the old eyes faded. 'Even if I go into remission, I don't know how long I've got so I'm grabbing at everything as fast as I can. I don't want to be sitting around when I've got weeks to go saying I wish I'd done that, wish I'd been there.' Henry drew a shaky breath. 'Get out there and live, laddie. This is your time. Now.'

Brad watched Henry strolling along to Reception, heard him giving Marilyn some cheek. Have some fun. Sure thing. With David wandering around on crutches and Erin having his baby, he struggled to find where the fun came in.

Laughter floated down the hall. Erin stood with Henry and Marilyn, *laughing*. He hadn't heard her doing that for days, weeks. One of the first things he'd noticed about her was how often she'd laughed with her colleagues, with her patients. But not recently. She hadn't had a lot of fun lately, either.

They needed to talk about the baby. Erin needed to know he accepted it was his, that he was ready to acknowledge that much, so why not have this conversation over a meal? Without thinking any more about it, Brad shoved his door shut and picked up the phone to punch in Erin's extension.

He heard her rushing past on her way to answer it and smiled. 'Hey, Erin, it's Brad.'

'Brad? What's wrong? Why have you phoned me? Or have we come so far that you'd prefer to talk to me with a wall between us?'

He refused to be put off. Phoning felt like fun. 'Are you doing anything tonight?'

'No-o.'

'Let's go out to dinner. I hear there's a great restaurant at one of the vineyards along Rapaura Road. Their specialty is seafood.'

'I can't eat seafood at the moment,' Erin muttered, but her voice was warming.

Or was that wishful thinking? 'Sorry, that was fairly dumb of me. They also have some other dishes that I'm sure will appeal. How about it? We do need to talk about the baby,' he added, knowing she'd find it hard to say no to that. Not the nicest thing to do but suddenly he wanted to go out with Erin more than anything he could think of.

'We won't go on the Harley, will we?'

'I thought you liked it.' She'd sure been excited by the time they'd ridden to Rarangi that day. Maybe she was afraid of getting excited again, of losing control of herself.

'I was thinking more along the lines of what I'd wear, and a dress is definitely not a good look on the back of a bike.'

A dress? As in a tight little evening dress? Brad's heart leapt against his ribs, and his mouth dried. What was this woman doing to him? He tried to swallow. 'I'll borrow David's car. So you'll come?'

'Have you ever known me to turn down a meal?' Then she faltered. 'I'm sorry, that sounded flippant. I'd love to go out for dinner with you, especially if we're going to talk about our problem.'

Yeah, they'd talk all right. But she'd better not get her hopes up too much. He didn't have a lot to say about the baby. There wasn't room in his life for a child, definitely no room in his heart for a little one. And he especially wasn't about to propose and start playing happy families. He murmured, 'That's a date, then.'

'We could take the Alpha Romeo. You can drive.'

Grab the opportunities. 'I'll walk down to your place at seven-thirty.'

Towards the end of the afternoon Brad wandered into Reception to pick up a patient file and found Marilyn and the casual office girl, Caroline, huddled over a magazine, commenting on a movie star's weird hairdo.

'What's that noise?' Marilyn raised her head, a twinkle in her eyes. 'You're not humming, are you, Brad?'

Was he? Yes, he had been. Damn. There wasn't a lot to be happy about. 'Maybe.'

Caroline shook her head. 'You need to get in tune. That's terrible.'

'I don't know,' Marilyn chipped in. 'It's better than his recent grumpy mood. Something's happened to cheer him up.'

Caroline's eyes widened. 'Got a hot date for tonight?'

Yes. 'Not at all.' Did the lie show in his face? 'What's not to be cheery about? It's a beautifully sunny day and we've nearly finished clinic.'

Marilyn and Caroline looked at each other and burst into peals of laughter. 'He's got a very hot date.'

'Have you noticed,' Caroline said to Marilyn, 'that Erin's been in a bit of a funk lately, too?'

Marilyn's eyebrows rose. 'You don't think they

had a lovers' tiff and now they've kissed and made up?'

Brad tensed. 'Now you're gossiping.' Erin had better not have overheard this conversation. She'd be mortified.

The women just laughed harder. He stomped down the hall but by the time he'd reached his office he'd begun humming again.

Why did he feel so light-hearted? Nothing had changed. There was still a baby he didn't want. Erin would be waiting for answers to a load of questions. Instead of humming, he should be planning strategies for the evening.

Caroline popped her head around his door, giving him a wink. 'You know everyone would be thrilled if you and Erin got together.'

If only she knew.

A message flashed on his computer screen. Mail. What the heck, no one needed him right this moment. He clicked on the icon and warmth spread through him. Sammy had sent him a photo. 'Look at you, my boy. Don't you look swanky?' Brad leaned forward. 'Holy mackerel. Is that a shiner you've got there?'

'Talking to yourself now?' Erin asked from his doorway.

'Come and look at this. Sammy sent a photo of him dressed in his football uniform.' He quickly read Sammy's message, full of spelling errors. 'Seems that he tackled a boy twice his size and got an elbow in his eye.'

I wish I'd been there to see that. And I'd have been able to reassure him his eye would be all right.

'He's quite the lad, isn't he?' Erin leaned over his shoulder, the familiar rose scent making him wish he could spin around and hug her.

'Just like his Braddy Daddy.' Pride trickled through him. Samuel was coping with life without him there on hand every hour of the day.

Erin backed away, rolling her eyes, smirking shamefully. 'Sure thing, big boy. Take all the credit.'

'Why not? He had to have got some of my good points along the way.'

'See you later. Don't be late.'

'Punctuality is one of my good points.' Why did she care if he was late? 'I'll definitely turn up.'

CHAPTER TEN

Erin brushed her hair until it gleamed, trying to ignore the butterflies flapping around in her stomach. At this rate she wouldn't be able to eat a thing.

A dinner date with Brad. What did it mean? Thank goodness he'd used the phone to ask her out, otherwise he'd have seen how he'd rattled her. It was hard enough trying to ignore the seductive tones of his deep, sexy voice that made her nerves jangle all the time. How had no one at work noticed her feelings for him? She went around like a cat on hot tin.

Even when he spoke to her in his oh-so-professional tone, her silly heart tapped a tango. A woman would have to be made of granite and sworn to the nunnery not to be affected.

A loud knock on her back door heralded Brad's arrival. Right on time. She swallowed around the lump in her throat and took one last look at her reflection in the mirror. The short black dress fitted perfectly. She ran a hand over her tummy. At least Little Blob hadn't started pushing outwards yet.

'Beautiful,' Brad murmured when she opened the door to him. 'You look absolutely beautiful. That dress suits you.' Then he ran his hand down her hair, reverence in his eyes.

Heat flowed up her cheeks. 'Thank you.' So they were starting out on good terms. Maybe they could keep the tone of the evening civilised after all. The butterflies slowed their frenetic pace.

Once settled at their table in the restaurant Erin asked, 'What's David doing tonight?' After Brad's vehement statement last week that he always had to be there for the older man, it seemed odd they were here without him.

'Henry Marshall's babysitting.'

'I hope you didn't put it quite like that to David. He'd be appalled.'

'As if I would.' Brad put the wine menu aside. 'Red or white?'

'Sparkling water for me.'

He nodded in approval. 'Fair enough, though

one small glass wouldn't hurt the baby if you'd really like it.'

'I prefer to stay off the wine completely.' Her palms tingled. He'd mentioned the *B* word. 'I've stopped cycling, too.'

'That's not necessary. You can't wrap yourself up in cotton wool until the baby's born.'

'I want this child more than anything. And if that means giving up other dreams then I will. Cycling can be dangerous.'

'You need some exercise. It's all very well not going out on your bike any more but you can't stop moving completely. Speaking as a GP, naturally.'

The waiter loomed over them. 'Can I take your orders?'

Erin studied the menu and decided on Thai beef salad.

'And sirloin for me, rare.' Brad handed back the menus.

'Man food.' Erin tried for a smile.

'Yep.' Brad settled with one arm draped over the back of his chair. 'How are you keeping? I've heard you being ill a couple of times. Not getting too tired?'

Did he want her to hand in her notice? Was that what he was angling for? His questions brought the tension that kept her muscles tight and her stomach churning all day slamming into her again. 'I'm fine. The morning sickness isn't too bad. And, no, I haven't noticed being too tired.'

'Early days, I guess.' His eyes were fudge coloured tonight, warm and friendly. Not even her snapping at him changed that. 'But later on you might want to consider cutting back your hours. If you do, I'd like some warning so I can find your replacement. We'll need to think about another full-time nurse anyway once the baby's born. You won't want to be working then.'

'Hello, do I get a say in any of this?' Her blood started to boil.

'I thought you'd want to be a full-time mother.' Surprise raised his voice, causing the couple sitting at the next table to pause in their conversation and look over.

Keeping a lid on her anger, Erin said tightly, 'I have to keep working. While I don't have a mortgage and have a small investment, that doesn't mean I don't need an income. And children have needs that cost money and this child is not going without.' Her hand shook when she lifted her glass of water. 'But more than that, I love my job. Everyone's like my family, always looking out for me, having me around for meals.' Better than her real family.

'That won't change. In fact, I'd bet that once they all know there's a baby on the way you'll get even more attention,' Brad said. 'And relax about the financial side of things. I did say I'd help with that. I accept this is my child. I've got plans to open a trust fund as well.'

She gulped, and a bubble of water blocked her throat. Hastily covering her mouth with her napkin, she stared at Brad over her hand. What a turnaround. Then the words spewed out. 'You've accepted the baby is yours to the point you're thinking about investing in its future? When did you come to the conclusion I hadn't tried to trick you? Huh? Thanks for telling me. It's been an absolute laugh all week at work, edging around you like I was walking on eggshells.'

His Adam's apple bobbed. 'Hey, I'm sorry. I

didn't think of it like that. I should've talked to you earlier than this.'

As an apology it was pathetic. But they had a lot more ground to cover so Erin restrained herself. 'What other involvement in Little Blob's life have you decided on?'

'Little Blob?' His sensuous lips twitched. 'You're naming our baby Little Blob?'

'In the meantime. I prefer that to saying "it", which seems faceless, sexless.' She shrugged. 'Crazy, I guess, but I'm bonding with Little Blob.'

She jerked when Brad's hand suddenly covered hers. 'I love it. And you're not crazy. Little Blob it is.'

The waiter arrived with their meals, giving Erin a reason to pull her hand away. Running the back of her hand down her cheek, she softened towards Brad. This was a very different Brad from the man she'd begun to get to know. Tonight he seemed to be trying to deal with the situation instead of reacting defensively.

Did that mean she had to be even more alert around him? Was he setting her up for a fall? She swallowed a mouthful of beef and asked, 'How's your steak?'

'Perfect.' He smiled. Then started a completely ordinary conversation that had nothing to do with babies. 'Why did you choose Blenheim to settle down in?'

'I'd spent time here on exercise at the air force base and always liked the area with its endless vineyards and fantastic weather. The fact that the town is small really appealed. I wanted friendly and personal as opposed to a large, sterile city where no one has time for their neighbours any more.' She chewed thoughtfully. 'It's a great place to bring up a child. Not that I thought I would be.'

Whatever they talked about they always came back to the fact they were pregnant.

Brad coughed. 'Some might disagree with you. I had a terrible upbringing in this place, turned into a thorough tearaway. It really is true that I could've easily ended up in jail.'

'But you didn't because of the kind of people who live here. People like David and his wife.'

'They noticed me because I stole their car and wrote it off slamming into a bank.'

'Your driving skills needed work.' Suddenly relaxed, Erin grinned.

And Brad gave her a return smile. 'One of the first things David did was take me up the Wairau Valley onto the gravel and taught me how to get in and out of trouble with a vehicle.'

'Is that what you'll teach our child when it's old enough?'

Instantly Brad's smile disappeared, replaced with a grim expression. Erin's stomach sank with foreboding. She shoved her plate aside, reached for her water only to find the glass was empty. Why hadn't she kept talking about neutral subjects? *Because I need to know these things, want to understand what role Brad is going to play in our child's life.* Heard of giving a guy a break? Being patient? He had taken her out to dinner. He had told her he'd help financially. Why did she have to go and spoil the easy atmosphere that had settled over them?

Brad drained his wine glass, pushed his empty plate away. Nodding to the waiter, he ordered two coffees, before picking up the conversation again.

'Erin, I think you missed the point. I still don't intend getting involved with this child.'

'But—'

He held his hand up to stop her saying anything. 'Losing Sammy was excruciating. If you were to take this child away from me, I doubt I'd survive the pain.'

'Why do you think I'd do that?' Erin's heart was thudding in her ears. This was so important for all of them and yet she didn't know how to get through to him, to prove to him she'd never take Little Blob from his or her father.

Brad stretched back on his chair. 'Have you thought about what will happen when you get married again? There'll be another man in the picture, living in the same house as you two, sharing meals, picnics, parties. With the best of intentions I'll still end up on the outer edge of my child's life.'

His eyes pleaded with her to understand. She didn't. Not entirely, despite the hurt she knew he'd suffered over Samuel. 'I hear what you're saying but I'm not your ex. I'd make sure your relationship with Little Blob was paramount. Besides,

I'm not getting married again.' She loved Brad and there'd be no wedding with him.

'You mightn't think so now, but one day you'll meet a guy who loves you as you deserve and wham. Wedding bells.' His hand slapped the tabletop, making Erin jump. 'And there goes my child. Off with another daddy.'

She saw his point. Even allowing that she'd make sure their child had all the access in the world to Brad, the child would be living in two families, with two fathers. Not ideal, for anyone. 'I am not getting married again. End of story.'

'How long were you and Jonathon married?'

'Four years.' Not that long at all.

'What happened? I think you've mentioned something about an accident.' Brad subjected her to an intense scrutiny.

She studied her glass. 'A car accident.' Because he was speeding home to her. 'Like me, Jonathon was in the army. The week he died he was away on exercise. We'd been trying for a baby for ever and were having infertility treatment prior to starting IVF. But I kept hoping we'd get there on our own, and of course my cycle didn't wait for the army.'

Brad nodded. 'So he was coming home to make a baby.'

Her eyebrows rose. 'That's exactly what he was doing.' She twisted her glass back and forth between her hands. 'I blamed myself. I was desperate to have a child, and couldn't face missing another month just because Jonathon was away playing army games.'

'You pressured him to come home?' His brow creased, his eyes were thoughtful.

'Yes.'

'Didn't your husband want a baby?'

'Of course he did.' She'd never have gone through all that stress of trying to get pregnant if he hadn't. 'He felt I was getting obsessive about the whole thing but he still left the exercise and drove three hundred kilometres for me, for us.'

'Except he didn't make it.'

She'd waited for hours, pacing back and forth in their tiny army house, growing colder and more worried by the hour. 'The police believed he fell asleep at the wheel. Hardly surprising considering he hadn't had any sleep for the previous forty-eight hours.' Her coffee tasted bitter. She placed the cup back on its saucer. 'They found the car immediately, in the Buller River. Fishermen found Jonathon's body five days later, downstream snagged in tree roots.'

An image of Jonathon in the morgue rose before her eyes. Cold, white, gone. She shuddered. Whispered, 'I shouldn't have asked him to come home. I'd been on enough exercises to know that everyone worked long and hard for days on end, that no one ever got enough sleep.'

Brad covered her hands with one of his. The warmth didn't touch her sudden chill. 'It wasn't your fault.'

'Yeah, I finally worked that out after years of punishing myself. I thought if I hadn't insisted on treatment that month he'd still be alive. I *was* getting obsessive about the whole deal and we'd argued before he left on that trip. I think coming home was his way of making it up to me.'

Brad squeezed her hands gently, pushed his chair out from the table and crossed his legs. 'Jonathon made a choice. He could've stayed on exercise, but he chose to come back to you. I assume he wanted that baby as much as you. If that was me, I'd have done everything I could to make it happen. Even knowing I was overtired I'd have driven back to you.'

Yeah, he would. He cared about the important things.

The next morning Brad watched Savita ease down onto the chair in his office and lift a sleepy toddler onto her knees.

He asked, 'Who's taken your place in the store?'

'My husband's managing while I'm here. But I bet Mum will be there by the time I get back. She'll want to know everything you have to say.'

'Next time bring one of them with you, if you like.' Brad glanced at the little boy curled against his mum, his thumb pushed into his mouth. Sammy used to do that. 'How did you manage when Mally was so ill?' He'd been reading up on Savita's notes and learned about her family history of heart disease in their newborn babies.

Savita shrugged. 'Sometimes I ask myself that

question. But when you have no choice you just get on with it.'

'Well, I hope you don't wear yourself out with this pregnancy.' A baby as well as a toddler and a busy shop to run didn't bode well for a relaxed, stress-free mother. 'How about organising someone to come in and give you a break every day?'

Savita's eyes snapped wide. 'Why? Is there a problem? Did my tests show the baby's ill? Like Mally was?' Her hand tightened on her son's arm and he grizzled sleepily.

Brad cursed under his breath, regretting how he'd worded it. Lately he seemed to lose concentration at the most inopportune moments. 'Sorry, Savita. No, there's absolutely nothing wrong with your bloods. They show you're very healthy and that you're eight weeks along.'

But the woman before him didn't relax. 'I need to know the baby hasn't got a hole in its heart like Mally did. Can you find out for me?'

'We will be monitoring you and the baby's growth all the way through this pregnancy. I've talked to your previous paediatric cardiologist and he'll be advising me along the way. He also wants you to go over to Wellington later in your pregnancy so he can do some scans.'

'Thank you. I don't know what I'd do if we had to go through the same thing again.' Some of her panic subsided, but her hands kept picking at Mally's jersey. 'It's terrifying thinking about it, you know?'

'I can understand that.

Savita was still talking. 'I guess if there's something wrong with the baby then we'll cope like we did last time.'

'You're incredibly brave.' Did she really think she'd be able to manage? The stress would be immense. 'But I suggest you try not to worry about it. We'll deal with whatever arises when it happens.' Brad looked hard at his patient. 'Can you do that?'

'Not a lot of choice, is there?'

Brad slipped the blood-pressure cuff around her arm, began pumping the bulb to inflate it. 'You seem more accepting of the pregnancy than you were last week.'

'It was a shock, I don't mind admitting. Took a

bit of getting used to the idea of another child but my husband's so happy I can't stay upset.'

Brad concentrated on taking the pressure figures. 'A little fast but nothing to worry about. Probably due to you rushing to get here and being nervous about everything.' He gave a reassuring smile, and asked, 'So he doesn't have any worries about this baby?'

'Of course he does, but he'll cope the same as me. We love children and until Mally was so sick we'd always intended having a big family. This pregnancy might be an accident but it's a good thing, otherwise we might never have had more children. That would've been really sad. Families are so important, and I won't be short of help if the worst happens.'

'They are very important, and can be supportive.' Except his experience had taught him differently. Or had that been his fault? According to Penelope he had never been around enough, always working. Couldn't argue with that. Nothing had changed. He still worked every hour available, and when he wasn't working or doing something for David he was organising sports for the kids he'd collected into a team.

Who would be there for Erin? Even with a perfectly healthy baby, being a single parent involved a lot of work and devotion. She'd manage, for sure, but it would be exhausting. Also stressful with no one to share her concerns with. Could he be there for her? Take some of the burden off her?

Brad swallowed around the sudden lump in his throat. Talk about being selfish. So busy protecting his heart he hadn't stopped to think how that would affect Erin. But what about going back to Adelaide? He still hadn't completely decided what he was doing there. Damn it, when had he become so indecisive?

'Dr Perano, are we all done?' Savita brought him back to the room and his work.

'I'd like to examine you, if you don't mind. I'll call Erin in to look after Mally while I'm doing that.'

He found Erin in her office, gazing out the window, her hand cupping her almost flat tummy, a dreamy expression on her face. The lump returned to his throat. She was beautiful. Even facing pregnancy on her own, and the worries she must have regarding being alone, she looked wonderful.

Without thought, he strode into the room and wrapped his arms around her, tucked her head under his chin. 'Hey, how're you doing?'

She stiffened, twisted around in his arms and tipped back to get a good look at him. 'I'm fine, Brad, perfectly fine.' She looked pointedly over his shoulder at the door. 'We're at work. Someone might see you.'

He deserved that for the way he'd treated her. 'You know something? I don't care.' And he dropped a kiss on her creased brow before letting her go.

'What's brought this on?' Caution slowed her words.

Which reminded him he had a patient waiting. 'Savita's here for a check-up and I need you to come through and hold Mally while I examine his mum.'

Erin smoothed her blouse down on her waist. 'Let's go.' Disappointment threaded through her voice. Had she been hoping for more from him? Of course she had.

He caught her arm as she started walking out of the office. 'Savita's been talking about her family. How they help out at the shop, and how they were there when Mally was so ill. She's very worried about this next baby but says she'll cope no matter what happens because of her family.'

Erin turned and locked gazes with him. 'So?' Her tongue skidded across her lip. 'What does that have to do with you and me?'

'Who's going to be there for you and Little Blob?'

'I've got friends.' She shrugged eloquently as though trying to underline her statement. 'Anyway, I'll be okay. I've got family, too.'

'In Australia.' His heart slowed. She wouldn't go over there. Would she? That would be ironic. Erin moves to Australia and he stays here in Blenheim. She had to stay here. He'd miss her so much. And that wasn't about the baby. That was because she'd crept under his skin when he wasn't looking. But he had no one else to blame if she did go.

'Relax, I'm not likely to go home to my mother.

She wasn't very hands on bringing me up, and she's not going to be any better with a grandchild.'

'Don't they care about you?'

'Yeah, they do in their own aloof kind of way.' Her sigh filled the air between them. 'But I hope I do a much better job of parenting.'

'I know you will.' He meant it, totally.

'Thank you. I think.' The surprise in her eyes touched his heart, made him swear silently he'd do more for her in the future. As long as he could find a way to keep the baby at arm's length.

Then he surprised himself, asking, 'Interested in having dinner with me tonight? I'll cook something on the barbecue.'

'David and Henry hitting the town together?'

'It seems so.' He didn't add that both men thought he should be getting a life. One that involved Erin in particular. 'So, what do you say?' Probably no, considering how the last meal they'd shared had gone. But he wanted to make it up to her, to show he wasn't always such an oaf when it came to difficult situations.

'Could we make it tomorrow night? I'm babysitting for Annie and Rick tonight.'

'Not a problem.' He squashed his disappointment. Tomorrow night seemed eons away.

'Then, yes, thanks, but can you promise not to go around here humming? You gave the staff the wrong idea last time.'

'Yes, I did, didn't I?' Except it hadn't been wrong. He enjoyed Erin's company, loved the way she tackled problems head on. 'Can I whistle?'

Her eyes rolled. 'Let's get back to Savita. She'll be thinking you've forgotten her.'

He had, briefly. It was a worry that he could be distracted from his work so easily.

But before Erin could move he dropped a kiss on her forehead. Breathing in her scent, he smiled. 'We'll work this out, promise.'

And he started humming.

CHAPTER ELEVEN

'THANKS for seeing me, Doc.' Jasper grimaced with the pain coming from his sliced hand. 'We thought it would be quicker to come here than go to the hospital. Little Dylan will be hungry soon and Suzie doesn't like breastfeeding in public.'

Brad looked at the couple sitting before him and shook his head in amazement. They really had got it all together for two people aged only eighteen. Their son was seven days old and Suzie looked like she'd been having babies for years. 'Not a problem.'

He'd been about to lock up and go home when these two had banged on the door in a very insistent manner. Unwinding the blood-soaked, makeshift dressing on Jasper's hand, he asked, 'How did this happen?'

'I was cutting a pumpkin and it spun out of my

hand.' Jasper sucked air as Brad examined the wound.

'Nothing a few stitches won't fix. I'll give you a local to numb the area.'

Suzie teased her partner. 'Don't think this gets you out of doing the dishes, hotshot. Or changing Dylan's nappies.'

'Come on, that's got to be dangerous. I might get an infection.' Jasper looked at Brad. 'Help me here, Doc.'

Brad laughed. 'Wear a plastic glove and you'll be fine. I'll give you a handful before you leave.'

'Thanks a lot.'

Suzie grinned. 'Yeah, thanks, Dr Perano.' She jiggled her baby on her knees and blew a kiss on his tiny chest. 'Your daddy thought he could get out of the messy stuff.'

Waiting for Jasper's hand to go numb, Brad asked Suzie, 'Any problems with Dylan? Anything you want to ask?' But truthfully the baby looked a picture of health, very well cared for.

Suzie and Jasper both shook their heads. 'Don't think so.'

'Everything seems to be going along as it

should.' Suzie's adoring eyes flicked between her child and Jasper. 'No problems, eh?' Then she startled Brad. 'Do you want to hold him?'

The proud mother held her son out to him, giving him no choice but to place his big hands around the tiny baby and lift him over to his lap. The sweet smell of freshly bathed baby tickled his nostrils and brought a raft of memories flooding in. He'd loved bathtime with Samuel. Lots of splashing and high-pitched shrieks. Samuel fighting the clothes Brad tried to dress him in, wanting to be free of the constraints of a nappy and singlet, kicking his tiny, perfect feet in the air.

He bounced Dylan on his knee and got a gummy grin for his effort. Brad's heart lurched. Another thing he'd forgotten was those grins, brought on by wind more often than not, but heart-twisting all the same.

'Isn't he cute?' Suzie asked.

'He certainly is.' Brad studied the serious eyes regarding him from his lap. There was something special about babies. Their innocence was like a whiteboard waiting to be written on. What would these two teach their son? What would they expect from him as he grew up?

What would he teach his own child? What would he expect from her? Because it was a girl. A little Erin, he was sure. Shiny black hair and sensational blue eyes that would look at him as though expecting his very best input into her life. What did any of this matter if he wasn't going to be around for her? If he kept insisting on having nothing to do with the baby?

'We just love him to bits. I wouldn't trade places with any of my friends,' Suzie told him.

'My mates think we're bonkers keeping him, but they don't know what they're on about. How could we adopt him out? He's ours, a part of us. We probably won't ever have much money but who cares? We've got Dylan. Look at the little blighter so happy with you holding him.'

And Brad did look. Closely. At a very contented baby. Despite their cheerful affirmations it couldn't be easy at their age. All their friends would be out having fun every weekend while they'd be tied down with a baby and no money. Yet they were unfazed.

Dylan burped, and dribble rolled out one corner of his pink mouth. Reaching for the tissues on his desk Brad gently wiped up the mess. Warmth stole over him as he sat watching the little boy. Oh, yes, he remembered doing exactly this with Samuel; remembered the peace that would steal over him when holding his baby after a particularly horrendous day at work.

Brad's world tilted. He was making a huge mistake by refusing to be a part of his child's life. If something went wrong, if Erin took their child away, then he'd deal with it. Somehow he doubted she'd ever do something so callous. But unless he took part in bringing up their child, unless he committed himself to being as good a father as he possibly could, he'd lose out anyway.

By your own actions. Not someone else's.

'I can't feel a thing in my hand, Doc,' Jasper interrupted his musings.

'Right, let's get on with it.' Brad passed Dylan back to Suzie's eager arms, and concentrated on stitching the wound in Jasper's hand, humming as he went.

A squiggle of hope wormed into his heart.

He could be a dad. The squiggle grew. Another chance to be part of a family. He and his child. Half a family. The hope diminished. He couldn't take the child away from Erin. But they could easily share custody. With Erin living next door it would work well. He could babysit either at David's or at her place if she wanted to go out. He'd be available when needed but never get in Erin's way.

A perfect solution. So why wasn't he smiling? He'd have to convince Erin of the merits of his plan. That might be harder than making beans on toast without the beans. Or would it? He'd discuss their future and that of their baby with her tomorrow night.

After seeing the young family out, Brad returned to his office and picked up the phone. Punching in the numbers that would connect him to Samuel, he leaned back and put his feet up on the desk.

'Hey, buddy, it's Braddy Daddy.'

'Braddy, cool. How come you're phoning today? It's a funny time, too. Did you know that?'

'I didn't even think about it. I just wanted to see how you're going? Tackled any more big guys?'

Samuel giggled. 'He's my best friend now. We went to the movies last Monday after school.'

Brad grinned. He loved that giggle. 'You sound really happy.'

''Course I am. You phoned me. I love your phone calls. I do miss you, Braddy, but I love living in America. It's a cool place. I've got lots of friends and school is getting better now that I've got a new teacher.'

'I'm glad, Sammy. You've got to be happy wherever you are.' Hello? He hadn't set a very good example. But where was the disappointment that Sammy was happy? That he wasn't broken-hearted because they weren't together?

'Braddy, do you still miss me lots?'

Brad swallowed. 'I sure do, son. That's why I phoned.'

Sammy giggled again. 'You can phone me every day if you want. I'll always be here. Oh, except on Tuesday nights 'cos I've got football practice, and on Wednesday I go to gym, and Friday we eat out at the Robin Nest diner.'

Suddenly Brad felt laughter bubbling up through his chest and onto his tongue. This was okay. He wouldn't lose his son completely. They had a connection. 'I love you, and I'll phone heaps.'

'Love goes everywhere, Braddy.'

Brad couldn't answer for the lump in his throat. He listened to the phone click off at the other end and sat staring at absolutely nothing. But in his mind was an image of Erin, laughing as she offered herself to him.

Love goes everywhere, Braddy.

It was time to tell Erin he wanted to be a part of their child's life. But more importantly, it was time to tell her how much he loved her. A life without Erin didn't bear thinking about.

Erin dragged herself inside to her kitchen. Dumping the heavy recyclable grocery bags on the bench, she headed back to the garage for another two bags in the car. Lucky streaked ahead of her, nearly tripping her up.

'Hey, watch it, missy. I'm not feeding you until I've unloaded this lot.'

Lucky wound around Erin's feet, effectively halting her mistress.

'What's all this smooch stuff?' Erin picked the cat up and cuddled her. 'How's your day been? Mine was okay, if you're asking. Brad's cooking dinner for me tomorrow night. Why do you think he's doing that?' She hadn't been able to stop wondering ever since he'd asked her to join him.

Lucky snuggled her head under Erin's chin and the purring got louder.

'Thanks a bundle. You're so helpful.'

Purr, purr.

'I'd better get moving. Annie won't be pleased if I'm late for my babysitting duties.' Placing the cat back on the floor, Erin quickly finished unloading the groceries and put them away.

'Now I've barely got time to change my clothes,' she told Lucky as she spooned tuna into the cat bowl. Hopefully Annie had something in her fridge she could munch on. Stripping off her work clothes, she shivered in the cold evening air. In a month or two there'd be snow on the far hills and ice on the roads. Tugging on jeans she hadn't worn since last winter, it surprised her to find they didn't meet in the middle.

'Would you look at this? Little Blob's not so little any more. I'm going to have to get a new wardrobe.' Her hand curled over her slightly bulging tummy. 'How's it going in there, kiddo? Warm and cosy?'

Excitement trickled through her. She was going to have a baby. She punched the air. Yes. 'I'm going to be the best mum in the world. I'll love you to bits and we'll have so much fun as you grow up. I can hardly wait for you to arrive.' She grinned down at her stomach. 'But what am I going to wear tonight?'

Rummaging through her wardrobe she found a pair of loose cotton trousers. 'Hardly warm enough but they'll do.'

A quick glance at the bedside clock and she was running. 'Sorry Lucky, but I've got to go. Have a nice night and don't let every tom in town come visiting.'

She whirled around, raced out of her bedroom, slowing only to snatch up her handbag from the top of the stairs. Lucky ran with her, then veered across her feet. Erin tripped, toppled over the top step. She grabbed at the balustrade, missed. Spun her arms in an attempt to force her body upright, failed completely. Her body crashed down, bounced and slid all the way to the bottom.

Agony ripped through her. Her ankle twisted under her backside. Her arm wrenched in its socket, agonising pain shot through her abdomen. Then her head slammed into the floor at the bottom of the stairs and the world blanked out.

'How are things with you and Erin?' David's eyes drilled into Brad as they sat eating dinner.

'We get along fine.' Brad chewed thoughtfully. He'd told Erin he didn't mind if their colleagues knew about the baby so he should be telling David. 'Erin's pregnant.'

David grinned at him. 'She must be over the moon, considering her history of infertility.'

'In case you missed the point here, it's mine,' Brad said as a blast of pride struck. Damn it, he was going to be a parent again, like it or not. And, actually, he did like it.

'And it's taken you some time to accept the idea.

That's hardly surprising, but I had been wondering what was going on. You've been so moody lately.'

Brad picked up the beer bottle, took a slug. 'It has taken time to get used to it, but now I can hardly wait.'

David said, 'Don't spend too much time thinking about it. Erin needs you now.'

And he needed Erin. He had so much love to share with her. 'There's something else. I've decided not to return to Adelaide so if you want we can come to some arrangement about the medical centre.'

David's fork clattered onto his plate. 'It's all yours. You have no idea how long I've wanted this, and not because of the Parkinson's. I always hoped you'd come home.' He stood and came around the table.

His shaking hand gripped Brad's shoulder in a familiar gesture that had always comforted him in the past and now brought tears to his eyes.

'Guess I'm a bit slow about some things.' Brad laid his hand over David's for a brief moment.

'Seems to me you're finally getting everything right.'

'If it's okay with you I'm going around to Annie's after dinner to see Erin.' To hell with waiting until tomorrow night to tell her how he felt. He'd held onto the past for too long because it was easier than facing the truth. The truth being that because Penelope had hurt him it didn't mean Erin would. And he had to take ownership of some the blame for his marriage failing. He had spent a lot of hours away from home. There was no undoing the past but he sure as hell could do something about the future. Especially if it included the woman who mattered so much to him.

When Erin had told him about the baby he'd hurt her, told her he wanted no part of it. He hadn't even given her a hug. His vision of babysitting the baby occasionally was only half a picture. Without Erin in it, at his side, it would never be complete.

The phone rang, loud and jarring, shattering the comfortable silence that had fallen between him and David. 'I'll get it,' he said. Not that David looked like moving anyway.

'Brad, is that you? It's Annie. Have you seen Erin?' Panic edged Annie's words.

'Not since she left the centre. What's up?'

'She's supposed to be babysitting for me. It's Rick's birthday and I've got a surprise dinner arranged. She should've been here half an hour ago. I've rung her land line and her cellphone but no reply. It is so unlike her to be late or out of contact.' Annie sounded breathless. 'I'm worried.'

A niggle of something akin to fear lodged in his chest. Stupid reaction. This was hardly a major alert. 'I'll go down to her house now. I'll call you from there. But relax. She'll be fine. She knows how to look after herself better than most.' But she was pregnant. That changed everything.

He ran. Tore through the trees and leapt over the back fence. Pounded on Erin's back door. Nearly broke the handle trying to open it. Locked. Around to the front. Relief. The garage was wide open. He barrelled inside calling, 'Erin, are you here? Erin, answer me?'

Silence. She wasn't here. Was that good or bad? But she wouldn't leave the garage open if she'd gone out. He moved quickly through the kitchen and dining annexe.

Meow. Lucky stood in the doorway leading to the front entrance and the stairs.

'Hey, cat, where's Erin?' Brad stepped over the cat and stopped. 'Erin? Hell, no. Oh, my God.' His heart thundered against his ribs as he dropped to his knees beside Erin's still body. His mouth dried as he found her carotid artery. His throat clogged with unshed tears when he felt the faint beat of her pulse.

Tugging his phone from his pocket, he leaned over to place a kiss on her cold cheek. 'Hang in there, babe. For your baby.' Then he dialled 111.

'Dr Perano, can you move to the front of the ambulance, please?' The paramedic pointed to the passenger seat.

Brad glowered at the woman and shuffled an inch or two along the second bed where equipment was strapped in place. He knew he was a pain in the neck but he refused to let go of Erin's hand, afraid she might slip away with no one holding her. She looked so pale and still that he struggled to believe she was alive. Being a doctor meant absolutely nothing in this situation. This was Erin. His Erin.

'Okay, I understand, but try and keep out of the way.' The paramedic reached up to check the IV saline level, then read the oxygen saturation level.

Up front the ambulance officer drove carefully so as not to jolt Erin, at the same time talking to the emergency department at the hospital. 'Thirty-year-old female, stat two, unconscious.' The monologue continued; professional, remote and chilling.

Brad's grip on Erin's hand tightened. Her face was immobile. Silently he willed her to open her eyes, wanted her to smile and say, 'Hey, what's the fuss about?'

She didn't. Brad's gut churned. He looked at the paramedic for the reassurance she couldn't give him. Instead she squeezed his shoulder in sympathy. 'She's lucky you found her when you did, Doctor.'

Erin's face was slightly distorted by the yellow plastic collar put on to prevent any movement of her neck. Given the nature of her accident, a damaged spine was a terrifying possibility. At the house when the paramedics had put the collar on he'd nearly freaked out. It had taken all his willpower to stay quiet, knowing it was a precautionary measure.

Hoping it was only a precaution.

Leaning close to Erin, he whispered, 'Hang in there, sweetheart. Be strong for me.' Though why she should give a rat's backside about him was hard to say. He hadn't exactly been obvious in his love for her. 'I mean be strong for our baby. Don't move at all. In case your spine is injured. You've got to keep absolutely still to prevent any further damage.'

'Baby?' the paramedic asked. 'Is Erin pregnant?'

'Yes. I told you when you first arrived. Didn't I?'

Tactfully the paramedic turned to her patient saying, 'Don't worry. There's nothing I can do anyway, but I need to note it down on the patient report form. How far along is she?'

Brad watched Erin as he answered. She hadn't moved a centimetre in the whole time since he'd found her. Not even her eyelids had lifted. It terrified him.

'Excuse me, Dr Perano, but we're taking Erin inside now.' The paramedic nudged him until he moved out of the way.

He had to let go Erin's hand for the brief time it took the crew to unload the Stryker bed from the ambulance, but he reached for her again the moment they began rolling in through the doors to ED. Her skin was cold, clammy, kicking his heart rate into overdrive. 'Come on, Erin,' he encouraged.

Her eyes dragged open, before fluttering closed again.

'Hey, Erin.' Brad's throat closed, preventing him saying any more. He tightened his hold on her hand, fear still thickening his blood.

The ambulance crew handed over to the ED staff, and Brad had his first glimmer of hope when he saw Andrew Pascoe talking to the head of ED, Roger Bailey.

Brad charged over. 'Andrew, you've got to examine Erin. She's nearly three months pregnant and she fell down her stairs. She's a mess.'

Andrew and Roger crossed to the cubicle Erin

had been put into. As she was transferred to a bed they read the ambulance report together.

Brad could feel his blood pressure rising. What were they dithering about? Get on with checking Erin over. She was unconscious and it was obvious from the angle her arm and ankle rested at that she had fractures. His gaze was drawn inexorably to the blood seeping through her trousers between her thighs.

'No.' Agony crawled up his throat and over his tongue. 'No, damn it.' It couldn't happen. Not to Erin. She didn't deserve this. Big-hearted, caring Erin could not miscarry. 'Andrew, help her.'

The gynaecologist gripped Brad's shoulder. 'I'm onto it. I know this is hard for you, man, but can you wait outside while we assess Erin's injuries?'

He was being kicked out? Away from his Erin when she needed him?

'She's unconscious, Brad.' Roger looked up from examining the wound on Erin's head. 'Priorities, okay?'

Outside the curtain Brad rocked from one foot to the other, silently begging the doctors to get on with it. He hated not knowing what was going on but sanity dictated that he would only get in the way if he returned to Erin's side. She needed help, fast. But she was haemorrhaging. Harming the baby? Losing it?

Brad rubbed his hands down his face. His fear intensified. For Erin. She'd be devastated if she lost her baby. From not being able to conceive to falling pregnant so unexpectedly had to have been a shock to her. But so often at work he'd seen a soft smile lightening Erin's drawn face as she'd slid her hand over her belly. She really wanted this baby. She mustn't lose it.

Just when Brad couldn't take another moment of waiting, Andrew slipped around the curtain.

'I'm arranging a scan immediately.' Andrew said no more. He didn't have to. Brad understood all too well the implications.

Erin tried to hold in a groan but the pain was intense. Her body felt as though a bus had driven over it. Her head throbbed with agony. Her arm ached, as did her ankle. Everywhere hurt.

'Erin? Are you awake?'

'Brad?' What was he doing here? She peered at

him through the gloomy half-light of her room. 'Am I in hospital?'

'Yes, you are.'

Her hand was being squeezed. Brad was holding her hand? She must've banged her head really hard. 'What happened?'

'I think you fell down the stairs.' His thumb rubbed patterns on the back of her hand.

She tried to recall everything, only got a fragmented picture. 'Lucky tripped me.'

'You were going to babysit for Annie. When you didn't turn up she rang me.'

'So you found me?'

'Yes.'

Her eyelids drifted shut. Why *was* Brad sitting with her? Was there something more?

The baby.

Her eyes snapped open. 'Brad?'

He was watching her, deep sadness etched over his face, darkening his eyes. Why hadn't she noticed the moment she'd seen him sitting there?

'My baby?'

Everything around her stopped. It was as though the world was waiting for his reply. Even her lungs stopped, her heart stilled. Except for her brain, where thousands of questions raced, where the one big question seared her, terrified her.

'Brad? Our baby? Tell me. It is all right. Isn't it? Everything's going to be okay. Please. Oh, God, please tell me the baby's all right.'

'I'm so sorry, sweetheart.'

'No-o-o-o.' It wasn't true. There'd been a mistake. She'd have a scan to prove the doctors wrong. Her baby was growing inside her, warm and safe. This was not happening. Not to her. Not to Brad.

Brad slipped onto the bed beside her, carefully bundled her up into his arms and gently held her to him.

So it was true. She'd lost her precious baby. Her miracle baby, the one she wasn't supposed to be able to conceive. The dream was over. Gone in a moment.

Brad's cheek rubbed against her face, his tears mingling with hers. 'I'm so sorry.'

'Has someone fed Lucky?' Erin asked in a monotone when she woke again in the middle of the night.

'You're worried about that cat? It's her fault you're in here.' If it was up to him, he'd strangle it.

'No, it was my fault.'

Warning bells went off. This sounded the same as Erin blaming herself for her husband's death. She could not do this to herself again. She might be a strong woman, but Brad didn't want to see her struggling with the belief she was somehow to blame for the loss of their baby. If she did then it could prove to be one tragedy too many for her. He took her cold hands in his. 'You can't blame yourself, Erin.'

'I shouldn't have been in such a rush. Stairs are dangerous.' There was no life in her voice, tightening Brad's stomach more than if she'd been ranting at him.

'If Lucky hadn't been at the top of the steps you wouldn't have tripped. If Annie hadn't asked you to babysit you wouldn't have been in a hurry. If it hadn't been Rick's birthday Annie wouldn't have asked you to look after the boys.' He squeezed her hands, shook them gently. 'There are a lot of ifs. This was an accident. You are not to blame.'

'How can you say that when you've also lost

your baby?' Her eyes were filled with sadness. And her damned guilt.

'Erin, I'm gutted about our baby.' He placed a soft kiss on her creased forehead. 'But you're safe. A bit broken and bruised, but you're going to be all right. That's far more important to me.'

Her mouth dropped open. Disbelief replaced the sadness and guilt in her beautiful blue eyes. Disbelief he could understand. He'd been superb at making her believe he wanted nothing to do with her and the child. By the time he'd come to his senses he was too late. The accident had happened.

She croaked, 'You don't really think that. You're just being kind.'

'Me? Kind? And I thought you knew me.' He'd tried for levity because her disbelief was killing him even when he fully understood where it came from. 'I don't do kindness.'

Tugging her hands out of his grasp, she tucked the sheet up around her neck and curled onto her uninjured side. Her eyes closed as though she was going to sleep but her teeth dug into her bottom lip, turning the skin white.

Brad shuffled his butt in the chair, trying to find a comfortable position, and prepared to watch over her some more. It was all he could do for her at the moment. He didn't want to look at the difficult times ahead as Erin accepted her loss. He didn't know how he'd see her through it, but he'd do everything within his power to get her to the other side of this tragedy.

When she finally drifted back into a drug-induced sleep he felt relieved not to see that dreadful agony staring out of her eyes. Her heart was in a thousand pieces. If he'd felt fear for her immediately after the accident, he couldn't put a name to what was roiling through him now.

Pulling the chair closer, he leaned his head on the bed as exhaustion overtook him. He should go home and grab some sleep. It was nearly dawn. But he wasn't leaving Erin. Not now, not ever.

This feeling of helplessness had little to do with the baby and a lot to do with Erin herself. She was everything to him. He loved her. Enough to marry her? Absolutely.

But now wasn't the time to be thinking about proposing. She didn't even know he'd decided to stay here. At the moment just knowing he wanted to spend the rest of his life with her lifted the black weight on his heart. That baby had been his hope for the future too. But Erin was even more so. Right now, and for as long as it took, he'd stick with her, see her through this. And if she didn't want anything to do with him at the end of that then he'd have to walk away.

He sucked in a lungful of air. Okay, he wouldn't walk away. Erin was a hearts-and-roses girl, despite her tough exterior. He'd shower her with those. She'd said she'd had a good marriage. He'd give her a better one, an exciting, love-filled union. But would she consider settling down with a screwed-up man like him? If he risked his heart by asking her to marry him, she'd probably pedal out of town so damned fast that he'd never see her again.

He was still going to take the risk.

He'd show her how much he cared for her with patience and love as her heart healed. He'd give her his all.

A whimper cut into his reverie. Glancing at Erin, he saw big, fat tears sliding down her cheeks into the pillow beneath her bandaged head. Even in her dreams she was hurting. His heart stuttered. Would she ever recover from this tragedy? Would she smile again, tell him once more to toughen up? Would she ride her bike races, striving not to be last amongst her friends?

If not, he'd still be at her side. Waiting, watching out for her.

Erin tried to roll over. Something heavy pinned down her good arm and shoulder. A dull ache throbbed everywhere, her arms and legs, her tummy. Her head pounded and her mind felt blurry. She was a mess.

Daylight was creeping over the windowsill. So she'd made it through the night without going screaming crazy with grief. She tried again to shift into a more comfortable position but still couldn't move. Tentatively raising her head, she groaned as the pounding became thumping.

Whatever held her down moved, pulled away.

'Brad?' She blinked at his beloved face peering at her. His cheeks were flushed with sleep, his eyes not fully open, his mouth crushed from the pillow. 'Have you been here all night?'

'I guess so.' He sat up, stretching and yawning, looking wonderful in his sleep-tousled state.

He sat up? Erin carefully turned her head sideways, and gaped. 'You moved another bed in here?'

'There wasn't enough room for the two of us in yours.' Brad made it sound so natural that he'd be sharing her bed if it had been big enough.

'They don't do king-size hospital beds.'

He yawned. 'I'm going to recommend them to the board. My arm kept getting cramp from reaching across to hold you.'

'Now I know what the deep rumble was that woke me up.'

'I don't snore,' he growled.

'Of course not.' Her heart swelled with love for him, the guy who didn't get within miles of people who might want to love him. But she couldn't believe for one moment he didn't blame her for what had happened. She'd heard his reassurances, but she didn't accept them.

For now she'd keep the conversation light. Far

easier than facing what had happened. 'What did the nurses say when they saw you'd rearranged the furniture?'

'They were great once I'd talked to them.'

'I can imagine.' Her fingers itched to run through his long hair. As she had that day on the beach. The day they'd finally given in to the heat between them and made love.

Made a baby.

Their baby. She slumped back against the pillow as pain filled her, engaging every part of her body. Her eyes blurred, her mouth dropped. Their baby.

Brad was instantly moving closer to her. 'Erin, love, come here.' He brushed her hair from her face with exquisite tenderness, then wrapped her up in his big, strong arms. His hand cradled the back of her head, his fingers gently massaging her scalp.

And her tears came. And came. And came.

Erin reached for her watch. Midnight. Her second night in hospital. Where was Brad? He'd been gone half an hour and she missed him already.

He was probably at home where he had David to worry about and his own bed to sleep in.

'Hey, you're awake.' The gruff voice she loved came from the doorway. 'I brought you a present.'

She watched as he came close. The front of his shirt bulged and he held it tenderly. Then he slowly extracted her present.

'Lucky?' A warm sensation tickled her. 'You sneaked Lucky in for me?'

He grinned. 'She nagged and nagged to come and see you.'

'You big softy.' Erin reached for her cat, cuddled her close, and rolled into a ball. 'Thank you.'

Maybe, just maybe, she'd get through this intact. Especially if Brad stuck with her.

CHAPTER TWELVE

Erin was running late for work. It was immunisation clinic morning and she had seven mums and their toddlers booked in to see her. She could only hope they'd be as forgiving as the group on her first morning working with Brad had been.

'Out of the way, Lucky, or you and I are going to have a serious talk.' Erin navigated around the cat and out of her kitchen, her arms laden with containers of food.

In the garage she placed her precious armload into the back of her car and returned to get more. In the kitchen she paused, smiling at the huge vase of irises sitting in the middle of her dining table. Brad had brought her flowers every week since she'd come home from hospital. Predominantly irises and winter roses, always beautifully arranged, they'd brightened up her home and pushed out the winter gloom.

Pushed out her own gloom.

Brad had been so attentive, so caring, since her miscarriage six weeks ago. She'd never have got this far without him. The pain of losing Little Blob was still there, fierce at times, but bearable now. The same pain was often reflected in his eyes, but whenever it became too bad for either of them they'd talk it through. Like a couple should.

A couple? Yes, that was what they were. Though neither of them had put it into words yet, that was exactly what they were. They'd grown so close since her accident they were almost inseparable. Brad had returned to her bed last weekend and at first their lovemaking had been poignant. Then it had been downright exciting.

Everyone at work teased them remorselessly now. At first people had tiptoed around her, afraid of upsetting her, not knowing what to say. But recently there'd been a lightening of the atmosphere at the medical centre. Erin felt more at ease with young patients. Babies no longer sent her into a torrent of tears. At least, not instantly and in front of everyone.

The phone rang, cutting through her daydreaming. 'Hello?'

'Are you coming to work today? Or do I need to send out for a new nurse?' Brad asked in that knee-bending voice of his.

'On my way. I've been baking up a storm as a way of saying thank you to everyone for their patience with me. Hope they're all hungry.'

'As it's nearly lunchtime they probably are.'

'It's not even nine o'clock yet so stop getting your boxers in a twist.' But she *was* late. And he was the boss, or so he liked to think. 'I'm on my way. See you in a few minutes.'

And she hung up before he could come up with any more smart comments.

He must have mentioned the baking to Marilyn because she was waiting on the back step when Erin zipped into the car park. 'Let me help you unload this lot. There are toddlers for miles inside, waiting for their favourite nurse.'

'Thanks, Marilyn.' She stacked containers into the other woman's arms and balancing the last two locked her car and raced inside.

The children crowded around her legs, pulling

at her skirt and demanding to be picked up. Each one got a special cuddle before their injection. Each one gave Erin heartache. They reminded her of her dreams for her child. They highlighted her loss. *Their* loss. Brad had suffered as much as she had. To have finally accepted he did want to be a father again had been a turning point for him. What followed had knocked him sideways, but he'd remained strong for her. Who knew what black hole she'd still be in if not for his fiercely protective love for her?

'They're all so adorable,' she muttered into Brad's chest when she sneaked into his office for a moment.

His hands stroked her back. 'They are, sweetheart, they are.'

'Why aren't I meant to be a mother?' She asked the question that frequented her mind daily.

'Hey, you don't know that you're not meant to be. Lots of women have miscarriages and still have children. There's absolutely no reason for you not to get pregnant again.'

'Apparently.' Andrew had told her exactly that on her last visit to the gynaecologist. Hearing him was one thing, believing was taking a bit longer.

Leaning back in Brad's arms, she asked the one question she'd avoided all along. 'Do you want a baby?'

There was only one man she wanted to have a family with. This man who held her as though she was priceless, treated her like a princess, and gave her a lot of cheek whenever he thought he could get away with it. If he really didn't think he could cope with a baby then she'd give up her dreams for him. Brad was more important to her than anything or anyone.

With his big hands he gently took her face and tilted it so he could kiss her. His lips were feather-light on hers. 'I can't think of anything I'd love more.' His kiss deepened and for a moment she forgot everything but Brad. Then he lifted his mouth away. 'Except you.'

'You say the loveliest things.' Erin snuggled in against him. 'You know I love you, don't you?'

'I guessed as much, but tell me again,' he teased.

Tipping her head back she looked deep into his fudge eyes. 'Bradley Perano, I love you with all my heart.'

'That's better.' His smile lit up his eyes. 'So when are you going to agree to marry me?'

He'd asked her twice already. Each time she hadn't felt ready. Hadn't thought Brad was really ready either. She knew he loved her but it still seemed like a knee-jerk reaction to the miscarriage. Overnight he'd done an about-turn on wanting his child and apparently on wanting to have a second chance at marriage. Erin desperately wanted to say yes, but something held her back. It was too soon. They needed to heal completely, start marriage with the tragedy firmly behind them, and at the moment she still got the speed wobbles around families.

Their turn would come. She had no doubt. But not yet. Rising on her toes, she kissed his chin, his mouth. 'Soon.'

He tried to hide his hurt, but his expressive eyes gave him away. 'Okay,' he murmured.

Taking his hands in hers, she kissed each finger. 'I do love you. I'm just not ready for this. I know I'm asking a lot of you.'

'It's all right, I promise. But once I want something I'm a very impatient man.'

'You think you're telling me something I don't know?' She grinned. 'Now I guess I'd better get back to work. Can't be skiving off with the boss whenever I feel like it.'

'I can't fault it.' He patted her bottom as she turned away.

'My coming in here? Or my bottom?'

'Both. Now go or I'll never get through all those patients waiting out there.'

'What a shame because it's nearly time for morning tea and all those yummy cakes I made.'

'Get out of here. I've got work to do.'

Early Monday morning, six months later

Erin looked up from her breakfast of bagels and strawberry jam to find Brad standing in the doorway. Her heart-rate sped up, feeling like she'd just cycled a one-hundred-kilometre race. And won. He looked so gorgeous—masculine, solid and trustworthy. And loveable. Completely loveable.

'How's that baby of ours?' he asked as he came right into the room.

'Very calm.'

'Not too quiet, I hope.' Worry tinged his voice.

'According to Andrew when I saw him last week, all is as it should be.' Erin paused, then asked, 'My scan's at nine. Are you still coming with me?'

'You've just saved me from having to gatecrash.'

'I wish I hadn't asked.' She chuckled. 'I'd love to have seen the technician's face when you burst into the room.'

'Are you sure we're not having triplets? You're eating enough for that many at least.'

She scrunched up her eyes and glared at him. 'Are you saying I'm getting too fat?'

Brad raised his hands, palms outward, his lips twitching. 'No way. My sense of survival is far too strong to say anything like that.'

Erin smiled, but a wee niggle of fear was worming its way into her heart. 'Brad…' She paused. 'What if there's something wrong with the baby?'

'Hey.' A large hand cupped her chin, tilted her head back. Brown eyes peered at her. 'Don't cry. We're in this together, remember? But I don't for a moment believe anything will go wrong. It wouldn't dare.'

Which was exactly why she was crying. Brad was so strong, supporting her through all her silly fears, never laughing at her.

Andrew was already waiting when they arrived

in Radiology ten minutes early. 'I think I'm as excited about this baby as you two are.'

'That's lovely,' Erin murmured.

'You're going soft.' Brad winked at her.

Erin was prevented from answering by the technician, Julie, introducing herself. Erin got onto the bed and reached for Brad's hand. She could barely contain herself. She was going to see their baby for the very first time.

As Julie applied cold jelly-like gloop to Erin's tummy she explained the simple procedure. Brad leaned over Erin's shoulder, his gaze glued to the screen. The intensity in his eyes made Erin smile. Already he was acting like a dad. She gave him a quick peck on his chin and turned to watch the screen too.

Julie lifted the wand away from her tummy and turned to Andrew, a question in her eyes.

Panic rushed through Erin, and her grip on Brad's hand tightened. 'What's wrong?'

Andrew answered instantly. 'Nothing at all.' He gave a reassuring smile. 'Everything looks very normal. You said you wanted to know so tell me, have either of you thought about what sex you'd like your baby to be?'

'Boy,' Erin said immediately.

'A girl,' Brad answered.

'I want a miniature Brad,' Erin reiterated.

'No, a miniature Erin for me,' came back Brad.

Andrew laughed. 'Then you're both in luck.'

Erin's head whipped around. 'What?'

'Twins?' Brad roared. 'Show us.'

Andrew took the wand from Julie and pressed it onto Erin's tummy. 'Look, there's your son, and your daughter is playing hide and seek behind her brother.'

Erin stared and stared. Hot tears streamed down her face. With everything that had happened, having twins was a bit much to take in. Twins. Oh, goodness.

'The start of our own rugby team,' Brad whispered.

Erin gasped, stifled a hysterical giggle. 'A cycling team.'

She barely heard Andrew say, 'We'll leave you two alone for a few minutes.' He must have gone, taking Julie with him, but Erin only had eyes for Brad. Now what? Two babies. Oh, my, this was going to be a lot to handle. Not that it mattered.

She could've been having quadruplets and she'd have been happy.

Brad looked as stunned as she felt. His eyes were fixed on the screen, which was now blank. Willing the babies' images back?

She joked, 'One each.'

Brad's gaze shifted to her, and then he leant over and kissed her. As his lips caressed hers she opened up to him, needing him, wanting to share this precious moment. He deserved all the happiness in the world. He sighed and wrapped his arms around her, then deepened his kiss. 'When we do things we do them big, don't we?'

Erin said, 'Did I mention I love you?'

'Four times on the way in.' He smiled a slow, delicious smile that lifted the corners of that delectable mouth. 'Now will you marry me?'

And even more months later

The Marlborough Express

Brad and Erin Perano are pleased to announce the early arrival of Kate and James, the first two members of their cricket team.

* * * * *

Mills & Boon® Large Print Medical

April

BREAKING HER NO-DATES RULE	Emily Forbes
WAKING UP WITH DR OFF-LIMITS	Amy Andrews
TEMPTED BY DR DAISY	Caroline Anderson
THE FIANCÉE HE CAN'T FORGET	Caroline Anderson
A COTSWOLD CHRISTMAS BRIDE	Joanna Neil
ALL SHE WANTS FOR CHRISTMAS	Annie Claydon

May

THE CHILD WHO RESCUED CHRISTMAS	Jessica Matthews
FIREFIGHTER WITH A FROZEN HEART	Dianne Drake
MISTLETOE, MIDWIFE...MIRACLE BABY	Anne Fraser
HOW TO SAVE A MARRIAGE IN A MILLION	Leonie Knight
SWALLOWBROOK'S WINTER BRIDE	Abigail Gordon
DYNAMITE DOC OR CHRISTMAS DAD?	Marion Lennox

June

NEW DOC IN TOWN	Meredith Webber
ORPHAN UNDER THE CHRISTMAS TREE	Meredith Webber
THE NIGHT BEFORE CHRISTMAS	Alison Roberts
ONCE A GOOD GIRL...	Wendy S. Marcus
SURGEON IN A WEDDING DRESS	Sue MacKay
THE BOY WHO MADE THEM LOVE AGAIN	Scarlet Wilson